Praise for M.S. Coe

"This coming-of-age novel, steeped in toxic masculinity and homespun rage, is as funny and disturbing as anything I've ever read. It's a sex comedy, road novel, and crime thriller all in one, rendered in deft and wicked prose that recalls Vonnegut, Atwood, and O'Connor. M.S. Coe is an uproarious and terrifying new American voice."

J. Robert Lennon, author of BROKEN RIVER

"New Veronia is masterfully crafted, Lord of the Fies-esque, stunning, and deep. No line is wasted."

Autumn Christian, author of GIRL LIKE A BOMB

"New Veronia is intense. As the early chapters develop, Coe develops complex psychological insight into the minds of and the power relations between Bennet, Toshi and Jay. The atmosphere shifts from early unease to a late terror, but a young and bungling terror wrought by teenage boys coming of age in an unforgiving milieu that, like Coe's book, never lets up."

Charlene Elsby, author of HEXIS

NEW VERONIA

M.S. COE

CL◀SH

For Will Cordeiro

Table of Contents

Chapter 1

I know for a fact that Jay came up with the shitty idea even though, later, Toshi tried to cop the plan as his. I've got a great memory; always have: I can remember my mother bending over infant me as I lay naked and sprawling on the blue checkered changing table, her tiny gold cross necklace dangling above my belly button, and I remember contracting my bladder, spurting the thin stream of celery-smelling urine out through my stunted penis and across my mother's face. Her lips and eyes flattened out, and her strangled scream (muffled by her closed mouth) sent a shiver over my skin. And I know that I remember this on my own, not in the way that a kid remembers something his parent told him about— which is less remembering and more internalizing "the story of when I peed on my mom as a baby"—but in my own, intrinsic elephant memory, because my mom left when I was two, and my dad and I have barely talked to her or about her since.

All this to confirm: Jay came up with the idea, and at first, it really was cool.

His inspiration arrived when Jay, Toshi, and I were sitting

around the kitchen table drinking Cokes. It was two years after the turn of the century, the start of summer, no school, flies droning above the sugared tabs we'd all flicked until they'd decapitated from the cans. Jay stared out the window that arched across the back of his house for a full minute before he shook himself.

His mouth hung crooked at the jaw: "What if we built our own little city?" The flies dive-bombed a puddle of Coke.

"Like a treehouse?" Toshi said. "Or a model? That's for kids."

"No, Knees—like somewhere killer. Super strong so even bears couldn't get in. A place girls would want to go."

Girls. At fourteen-going-on-fifteen, we all knew the power of the word.

"I mean, we could really make it." Jay opened another soda and bent the tab of the can back and forth, back and forth, until it popped free. "Build a cabin, a house. We could each have one. With a bed inside, a bunch of pillows."

"What about a bathroom?" Toshi said. "We can't make that."

"We could too. An outhouse, sort of, but put a real toilet in there, with a pipe that leads far away. You can flush it with a bucket of water. Easy." Jay sat back and folded his arms across his chest, a new move he'd perfected to show off his pumped biceps.

"No, not easy," Toshi said, and I silently agreed.

"How are we going to build all this stuff?" I asked, thinking of teetering walls that fell and crushed us into the sewage-saturated ground. "It would take forever."

"Listen to Soppy," Jay said. "Must be worried because his dick spouts like a hose. Always needs a whole toilet for himself."

"Screw you," I said. I loathed the nickname—*Soppy*—

that I'd picked up in third grade for no reason at all, practically right after I'd moved to Delaware.

"Bennet, come on, man," Jay said to me. "We have the whole summer. Don't be an ass-posit. What else do we have to do?"

"I'm supposed to go to camp," Toshi said, "even though last time, I got a spider bite that nearly made my finger fall off and then I couldn't even play the horn. In the US, six-point-six people die every year from spider bites."

"Get out of it." Jay sneered. "Band camp is for losers. It's the same old, same old. But this, this could be something new. This will get us some pussy." His hand shot up and snatched at a buzzing fly, but he missed.

―――――

That night, my dreams narrowed in on a specific pussy—Stella's—which floated hazily before my REM eyelids; pink and delicious-smelling like bubble gum, sort of rubbery, something I could stick my tongue into for that satisfying pop, then wrap against my lips to blow the bubble over again.

Stella, the most fabulous woman on the peninsula, was one year older than me, one year ahead in school. Her curly brown hair showed up gold in the sun. Jeans clung to her ass, the seam pressing up against her crack. She popped out tits at eleven, and that year my obsession rewired my brain so that I became addicted, craving her. One third of my life, Stella had been *it*. That summer when she grew tits, she sat on my lap. The rapturous feeling: an incredible welling up, my body expanding into the air beneath her squirming, the cause of my first real hard-on. Sunscreen all over her. Ever since, any time I smelled the stuff, I thought *sex*. Her neck when she pulled her hair up into a ponytail glowed like fresh milk; the sight of that knob atop her spine was the main reason I worked hard in school, to skip up into her grade for a couple classes so that I could stare at the back of her head, at the white part down the middle of her skull which divided her hair into two braids.

The thought of Stella was the real reason I decided to go along with Jay's plan: Stella had emerged from the same soup of DNA as Jay—they were siblings—and if I spent the summer building a cabin behind her house, I would run into her all the time. Maybe she would lay out in the backyard, triangles of fabric against her skin, the contrast of tan and not tan an image I could take home with me each evening.

The morning after Jay's idea about building a little village, Toshi and I showed up at his house and, without really saying it out loud, we all agreed to the plan.

"We got lots of work ahead of us," Jay said, "but we can do it. For a good cause." He disappeared from the kitchen for a minute and came back holding a two-foot-high American flag. The white stripes had cocks drawn in them, realistic looking, with hair on the balls and veins snaking the shafts, and I saw that the pussy village was Jay's new project.

Jay waved the penis flag beneath my nose. "We got to find somewhere to plant it. We'll plant it and do a kind of naming ceremony today, and then we can get started on construction. First we'll build a bear trap in case someone comes creeping around our camp."

"I hate naming things," Toshi said.

"Sin City," Jay said.

I shook my head. "Too many things are called that. It needs to be romantic. Don't you think the girls are going to want romance?" Wrought iron bridges, blue convertibles, and gondolas breezed through my mind. Stella would wear a tight, white sweater.

4

She wasn't home—when I'd arrived that morning, I'd pretended to need the bathroom and instead hunted all over for her—but asking Jay where she'd gone would be equivalent to falling over, lovesick, and I could only debase myself that way every once in a while.

I said, "What about… New Veronia?"

"Huh," Jay said, "where's Old Veronia?"

I shrugged. "There is none."

"That's stupid," Toshi said.

"No, I get it." Jay pointed at me. "Bennet is right: the ladies will want something that sounds romantic."

"Because girls are stupid," Toshi said.

Jay scratched his chin where goatee hairs sprouted out of pimples. "I mean, I guess New Veronia sounds okay," he said. "Yeah, sure. Unless I think of something better."

I nodded along as the shock of my idea validated by Jay lightened my head to a balloon on a string, bobbing.

———

In the third grade, when we were in Mrs. Brown's room, Toshi, Jay, and I formed an alliance around our shared interest in the class pet, an iguana. Ever since those days of scouring the playground for bugs to feed Dino, we'd been friends. Our dynamic started right then: Jay telling us where to look and what insects to snatch, and me and Toshi seeing which one of us could follow his directions better.

Toshi and I lived just down the street from each other, our block a couple of miles, an easy bike ride, to Jay's place. Picture Toshi: tall and skinny and Asian-looking from his mother's side only, straight dark bangs in his eyes, red or yellow or blue t-shirts over jeans that ride up a little, but even a little is too much in high school. His parents divorced, mom moved back to Singapore, the place she was working when she met Toshi's dad. The fact that neither Toshi nor I have a mother anywhere nearby is strange for suburban Delaware, and I think it sort of brought us together. Not that we would share a good cry over our lost mommies, but that we could throw each other a look across the classroom when the teacher lamented that obviously our mothers had never taught us all how to use a tissue.

Jay is white, like me and basically most of the kids in our class, but beyond that similarity, we are pretty opposite look-ing: I have dark, wavy hair, blue eyes, and compared to Toshi and Jay, I'm sort of short. Jay is even taller than Toshi, with a blond crew cut and squint-hard brown eyes. A year ago, Jay had looked more like me, but then he sprouted up, a bit gangly, but muscled, with a sometimes-deep voice, a lump in the center of his throat, hair bristling from his face, and a new smell like hardboiled eggs. Jay is the only one of us to have a tattoo: a geometric construction etched on the back of his neck. He told us once that it was the earth, then another time that it was a Hindu punctuation mark, and then he even said it was supposed to be a zebra's eyeball.

Jay's got this drive to stay busy, to always be *doing*, and so he spun projects out of thin air, a web that always caught me and Toshi. One time, he stole eggs out of chicken coops across the county, then pressed us into helping him sell them at the grocer's. When the man would not buy, the eggs ended up smashed across the glass doors of his store. In fourth grade, Jay documented every movement of a chubby girl named Christina. He kept this notebook on her—*scratched nose three times in a row, tapped heels of shoes together*—and used it to convince us that she was a witch. We ended up swiping a lighter from Toshi's dad and cornering her on the play-ground. Jay burned her on the forearm, to brand her as a sorceress, he said, as I stood guard and watched her scream. Remorse gave me a rash afterwards, and when Christina moved away in the sixth grade, I felt relieved that I would no longer catch sight of her in the hallway and be overwhelmed by a wash of guilt.

This particular project, New Veronia, seemed harmless, with its main goal literally constructive: who could we hurt while building cabins out in the woods?

Into the backyard we marched behind the penis flag; our pockets bulged with chips and sodas. The second-story window of Stella's bedroom hung open, red curtains jerking in the breeze, and I entertained a brief daydream of me climbing up there to find her naked on the bed. As the woods deepened around us, Toshi began to pause every few yards to pick up a rock or scratch at the earth with a stick. "Damp," he kept muttering, "damp, damp, damp." Probably he was worried about the dampness breeding disease. He would get these strange headaches—he described them to me once as a worm crunching slowly through an apple, and that apple was his brain.

"Keep it up, Knees," Jay said. "Find us a stable foundation for New Veronia and all that. Over there"—Jay pointed the flag east—"is this hillock thing. Let's go check it out."

The spot was maybe three-quarters of a mile off from the house, and as soon as I set foot on it, I knew that it was our place.

The woods in Delaware have tall, strong trees with branches that start high up and not an overabundance of undergrowth. Deer and squirrels and birds and skunks rustle the leaves, and the sky up past the branches is usually a cottony blue. The heavy air sits against your skin like sweat, and it smells like something is dying and being born all at once.

Toshi, who had been poking at the ground on our

hillock, stood up and said, "This might be as dry as we're going to find."

"Just the place to get our dicks wet." Jay whooped and started to climb a tree. He made the top in an instant. He was the most physical of us; he played soccer and challenged us to pushup contests. "Hey!" he yelled from the top of the tree. "Hey, I can see the ocean from here! We got ocean views! The ladies are going to love that."

"It's the bay," Toshi said under his breath. "Not the ocean." He paced among the trees, his steps aligned heel-to-toe. "All these trees are in the way," he told me. "We'll need to cut down a bunch of them. This is how pollution starts, you know: one tree makes almost two hundred and sixty pounds of oxygen in a year."

Jay jumped from the lowest branch; his body fell from the sky to the ground. "Looks like there's enough room for a little house over here, and one over here, and one here. We can make the bear trap right here."

I said, "Or maybe... we could build kind of like the polygamists, with one big house, but three separate entrances? A triplex, basically."

"Gross," Jay said. "Polygamists?"

"I saw a documentary. You get, like, eight wives for one guy."

"I don't want to share *walls* with you. Then you'll hear all the nasty stuff I'm into and get jealous." Jay humped the air.

Toshi came out from behind a tree. "You know, the triplex would need less materials. It would probably save time. Three separate houses will be way too hard. But one triplex... we'd just need to build it stable. We wouldn't want one wall to make our whole place fall down."

"Don't worry, Knees." Jay knuckled Toshi's head. "We'll build it good."

"Build it, and they will come," Toshi said. "Maybe."

"They will come so hard," I said, and the guys whooped with joy.

Once we all stopped laughing, Jay said, "Yep, this is it. New Veronia," as if he'd come up with the name of our town, and not me. He said it again, drawing the syllables out like a song, and then he lifted the flag and planted it deep into the hillock.

Chapter 2

The three of us had spent a fair amount of time out in the woods that surrounded every housing development in Delaware. Sometimes the woods came right into the backyards, like at Jay's fairly isolated house, where his parents didn't seem much interested in cultivating anything that resembled a lawn.

A month into the third grade, at our first sleepover, Jay, Toshi, and I took an old army surplus tent, some flashlights, and a bag of marshmallows out into the woods behind Jay's place and set up camp. The evening had riled me straight off: I had expected Jay's parents to introduce themselves, his mom to serve me dinner, his dad to check over our camping gear, but instead, the grownups were absent. The house felt inappropriate with just the kids running it, but exciting, too: there was no one telling us what to do. We ate a block of cheese, threw a cup of water on Toshi when he came out of the bathroom, and yelled through Stella's closed bedroom door that there were spiders crawling up through the toilet. At that point, she hadn't yet become the love of my life.

After we'd made it out to the campsite, Jay told the first ghost story. His father had been telling him tales about the

Zimzee for years by then, so he had a nice store to draw from. "The Zimzee," he'd said, "is a tall, skinny creature that looks like a man, but with tree bark for skin. All dark brown. He don't got a face, just holes where his face things should be, and his bark is covered in stuff that looks like moss. Only it ain't moss, because it's the dead skin of all the kids he eats.

"He wanders around in parks or maybe outside kids' houses and stands still until they get close. He looks like a tree, but not really like a tree, so the kids go up to check him out, and that's when he grabs them. He skins you real fast and then eats you; his mouth is like a wood chipper. And this crazy old coon, he hangs your skin on his body to dry cause he likes to turn it into beef jerky and chew on it later.

"One day the Zimzee was getting real hungry. From far off, he heard some kids' voices. It was these twins, Matt and Mirabel…"

None of us slept that night. Clearly I remember the sound of the crickets shifting each time a cloud passed over the moon (darkening the roof of our tent), as if their laments were tied to the sky. I peed inside our empty water bottle because I was afraid of outside, of the dark. After that first story, trying to scare each other with the Zimzee became our tradition, and when we got older, we didn't really tell stories anymore, but we'd say things like, "I hope that bastard gets eaten by the Zimzee," or, "That old man has some kind of Zimzee skin disease."

━━

On the first day of building New Veronia, Toshi arrived late. When he finally did show up, he turned pale as he told us that his dad wouldn't let him get out of camp, that he had to leave in two short days.

"You can't go," Jay said. "We need you for the building and everything."

"He must have a new girlfriend," Toshi said. "Dad always wants me to get out of the house when he has a new girlfriend. He likes them more than me, even if they're ugly."

"No. Shit." Jay paced among the trees. "We can't with just two. It will be way harder. What if a bear invades?" He kicked savagely at a bush.

Already, the idea of New Veronia had become our collective fixation. We *had* to build the little city; our summer depended on it. My blood pounded with worry that maybe the course of our whole lives would be ruined if our plan failed now.

Jay said, "I know: this is band camp. The only thing you do all day is play songs; that's the only reason you go. So I'll just break your arm."

"Ouch," Toshi said.

"I'm sure it would work: broken arm, no band camp."

I marveled at Jay: he always took things further than I could even imagine.

"You said yourself that you don't want to go," Jay reminded Toshi.

"It's always too hot there," Toshi said. "But it's hot here, too. Maybe camp won't be so bad…"

"This could work." Jay started stalking around the confines of New Veronia, grabbing a plank of wood, a hammer, a rock. "We'll set up a sort of station," he called over his shoulder. "You lay your hand across here, see? With a gap right under where we put your wrist, and then I just sort of—" He lifted the hammer up over his head and arced it down.

"Um," Toshi said, swallowing hard; he rubbed his wrist absently.

"Come on, Knees," Jay said. "This will get you out of camp for absofuckinglutely."

Toshi's knees were shaking. This wasn't the reason Jay called him Knees—it was some stupid thing because he was

Asian, like Chinese, Japanese, Taiwanese…—but this new twist on the nickname helped release the tension in my jaw. I laughed.

"But Jay," I said, "with a broken wrist, he doesn't do us any good, either. We need him to build stuff. He needs his wrists."

"Shit!" Jay pounded the flat of his palm against his forehead, mocking me. "He *needs* his wrists. To build." Birds in the trees above us squawked at each other and rustled their wings, sending a couple of leaves drifting down to the ground. "Think about it. One of his wrists is at least better than none of them."

"What if… what if we just pretend that he broke his wrist?" I said. "I have my old cast from a couple years ago. They sawed it off me and it just kind of fell away in two pieces, but I still have it. There's this sock thing that you can put over it, to hold it together and to hide all the signatures that say 'Bennet.' "

Toshi looked up from where he'd been staring at his toes. "Yes—sure—that's a good plan. My dad is afraid of doctors. We just tell him that I broke my wrist over at Jay's house, and his parents felt bad and they drove me to the hospital and took care of the bill. Dad is always going on and on about how I've got to be careful, he wouldn't take me to the hospital unless I were dying, blah blah blah. A couple of weeks ago, he drove a nail straight through his palm, but he just pulled it out and stuck a couple of band-aids on. His pinky doesn't bend down all the way anymore. Doctors are the worst, you know? A broken wrist would probably cost about a thousand dollars."

Jay pulled his fists away from his eyes, where they'd been pressing into the sockets. "You think it'll work?" he said. "Really?"

Toshi said that you couldn't be sure of anything, but I told Jay that yes, it would work.

Our New Veronia future again solidified: straight away we started to clear the earth in the big triangle that would hold our triplex. I'd drawn up plans the night before, and a pyramid-shaped house would serve us perfectly: each door could open into a different facing direction, and we would need to build the minimum number of walls.

FRONT VIEW .... AERIAL VIEW

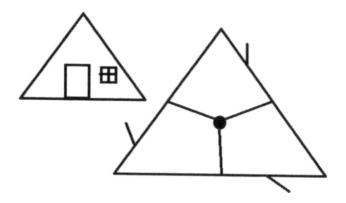

We would use one huge, old tree as the center post for the house, and we would build the walls out around it.

"Do you really think this will hold up?" Toshi asked. "It's not like you're an architect. They have to go to school for forever, the way you do for any good job, and so I'll probably be a landscaper, just like Dad."

"Looks good to me," Jay said, and so Toshi had to stop complaining.

We broke for lunch when the sun hung straight overhead. Jay peeled one of the bananas that Toshi had brought and held it in front of his shorts. "The guys told me about a new way of whacking off."

Whenever Jay talked about "the guys," he meant his high school soccer teammates. "You take a Styrofoam cup. You got it? And you fill it up with shaving cream and you put a lid on it. Then, on the bottom end, you cut a hole—it's got to be a perfectly round hole just about the size of your dick—and that's what you use. It's, like, pretty close to a cunt. When guys say *she creamed her pants*? It's like that."

"That would make a huge mess," Toshi said.

"Yo' mama creamed her pants." Jay shook his head. "Why am I even friends with you two bammers? Can't say a single yo' mama joke."

I said, "That's the sacrifice you got to make."

"Bennet." Jay threw his banana peel at me. "If you whack it to Stella, I will break off your dick."

I scoffed, like he hadn't caught me out. Jay always joshed me for being into his sister, and I always joshed him for thinking I was.

"She is such a cum dumpster," Jay said. "Been out with some guy all this week. My dad's going to have to marry her off fast as he can."

Jay always said shit like this, and even if it was true, it didn't make me like Stella any less: I'd heard that you didn't want two virgins having sex together, that it might not even work. Look at Adam and Eve: God commanded them to be fruitful and multiply, but Eve couldn't conceive until after the Fall. But Stella—she would know exactly what to do with my cock.

When we finished at the construction site for the day, Toshi and I left Jay and biked towards home. Without saying anything, we stopped at the Wawa along the way and each got a Styrofoam cup and a lid. You didn't have to pay if it wasn't full of soda. Then we biked to my place and snuck through the back door, into my room, where I unearthed my cast from the box of junk under my bed and fitted the two halves of it against Toshi's wrist. The plaster wasn't scattered with as many well-wishes as I had remembered, but there were notes from Toshi—*be more careful so this doesn't happen again*—and Jay—*guess your left hand will get in on the action now*. I fitted it to Toshi's wrist and wrapped it up with white athletic tape because the sock that had gone over the cast was lost, probably for the best, since it had smelled of old Swiss cheese. "How does that feel?" I asked.

"I think I'm getting a headache." He turned his hand over and then back. "Would Jay have really done it, do you think? Would he have broken my wrist?"

"Naw," I said, because I knew that Toshi needed to hear what he wanted to, and not what I really thought. "No way."

Chapter 3

The next morning, I caught sight of my face in the bathroom mirror. Somehow, it wasn't *me*, like I'd been bilked out of my regular skin and hair and eyes. Everything was growing rougher. My jaw was lined with spots; it was a new galaxy of whiteheads surrounded by red rings. Was my nose growing larger, or my forehead smaller? Black troughs from poor sleep shadowed my eyes, and my hair stuck to itself in greasy clumps. I squeezed milky worms out of my skin and worried that I might be inhuman, undead, rotting and maggot-infested. After my face was dotted with specs of blood, I checked the time and realized that an hour of my life had disappeared into that mirror. An hour: it had felt like a blink.

My dad was sitting at the breakfast table, which startled me until it dawned that it was Sunday; during the summer, I tended to lose track. He held his hair, which sprouted out from a bald patch at the crown, in both hands, massaging his skull, so probably he'd been out at the roadhouse the night before.

"So," my dad said, lifting his head so that I could see his reddened eyes (definitely the roadhouse), "summer."

"Summer," I agreed.

"What you been up to? You waste a whole can of my shaving cream?"

Jay's tip about making an artificial cunt from Styrofoam and shaving cream hadn't worked out so great. Thinking about Stella slowly unhooking her bra got me hard fast, sure, but when I slid my cock into the hole, I found that the Styrofoam, even cut into a perfect circle, felt sharp as teeth. I had to pull out after just a thrust or two and use my hand like normal.

"You guys got plans for the summer?" my dad asked.

"Don't worry," I said. "We're keeping busy." Then I thought about how Toshi was supposed to have broken his wrist the day before, but I kept my mouth shut, since my dad wouldn't find out anyway. He didn't talk with anyone much except his coworkers when they went out drinking. "We're fine doing our own thing."

He looked embarrassed, which was strange. Maybe he was finally getting the idea that I was growing up.

"Right," he said. "Long as you stay out of trouble."

Even though he probably would have been proud if I'd told him about building a sex fort out in the woods—he was always asking if I had a girlfriend yet and what I thought of Miss Lois Lane (his name for the high school math teacher) —I made up a lie about helping add a back patio onto Jay's parents' house for some extra cash. This impulse to tell him nothing about my life, to lie even when the truth was innocuous, had become essential to my self-preservation: if I was a complete mystery to my father, then he'd never be able to see through me to my obsessions. He'd never figure out where his shaving cream had gone or worry when I stayed out after dark.

"Well if you're working for someone else"—my dad poured himself another coffee— "then I guess you don't need an allowance, too."

"Dad, come on," I said, "Jay's parents hardly pay me anything. I'll still take out the trash here and all that stuff."

He looked at me, head lowered in a way that made the crick in his nose especially prominent. "Keep up that work ethic." He left before I could figure out if I would get my allowance or not.

———

"Today, we'll set the bear trap," Jay said. He was stretched out on the gray-carpeted floor of his bedroom; Toshi and I sat on the mattress above him. The place smelled as if the window hadn't been opened in years, and I'd moved up to the bed when I'd spotted a bowl sprouting a rainbow of mold on the floor beside me. Jay's house was always dirty, an alive kind of dirty, the sort of place you felt afraid to go barefoot in, and the whole atmosphere was closed off, unwelcoming. But the three of us always met up at Jay's.

"I scoped out the perfect spot for it. No asshole bear is breaking into *my* camp."

About nine months before, a couple of black bears had been spotted around our town. They slashed open above-ground pools and one of them ate some old lady's poodle. Delaware normally doesn't have bears, so their antics were plastered all over the news, and Jay made us hike around for hours, trying to find bear shit or claw marks or whatever. He rented videos about bear attacks, living with bears, getting eaten by bears, and he watched them over and over. I figured that the bears had probably moved on after realizing that Delaware wasn't so great, but Jay said he knew they were still out there.

"I bet we'll catch one before summer is over," Jay said. "I got a feeling."

The traps he'd dug up from his garage were heavier than they looked, and as I carried one to the site of New Veronia,

I kept my eyes on its metal teeth as the *Jaws* theme song played in my head.

"These things can snap a bear foot in two," Jay said as we dug holes to bury the traps' chains, "or at least bite really deep into the bone."

"This dirt is too hard." Toshi dropped his shovel and leaned back on his haunches.

"It'll make him real mad, to be caught like this." Jay stabbed a spade into the earth. "It would be so killer to have a bear coat. Like, a real hide coat, with a bear head for the hood."

After we buried the chains, Jay took the premade hamburger patties he'd raided from the freezer and circled them around, and then we scattered sticks and leaves over the whole thing, careful not to spring the traps.

"What if we forget where they are?" Toshi said.

Jay rolled his eyes. "Then I guess we'll have to amputate your foot."

When we came back the next morning, a swarm of flies hung over the hidden traps, and it smelled like old blood.

"This is gross," Toshi said, "and when we put a toilet in here, it will be even worse."

Jay poked him, hard, on the arm. "At least you won't step in the traps now. Your nose will tell you where they are."

I figured that our first step was to start chopping down trees for the triplex walls, but Jay said he'd come up with a better idea. "Pallets. The stores have them, tons of them, and they leave them out back for anyone. They're a whole huge source of wood! It's perfect. Way easier than cutting down trees."

"You think so?" It really was a good idea. Jay didn't have the brains for English or history or any of the other classes

I'd been in with him, but maybe he had a brain for building. That would be just like him, to surprise me after all these years. "Where do we get the pallets?"

"Stores, man, any store."

Toshi paused from unwrapping the tape around his fake cast. "The Save-Right," he said. "I know it seems far on the road, but if you walk straight across the woods"—he gestured with the blocky cast—"it's only a couple miles, maybe less, to get there."

"How do you know?" Jay asked.

"Sometimes I walk." Toshi shrugged. "I ended up there. It was easy. Not far at all. We drag the pallets from the back of the store, through the woods, to here."

I thought about the pyramids, how slaves had dragged those huge stones for miles so that the pharaohs would have amazing graves. But New Veronia would be better, because we'd get to occupy the pyramid that we built, and we'd be alive inside of it, a sort of alive I was really looking forward to figuring out.

"Let's get going," Jay said.

Me and Jay and Toshi jammed water bottles in our back pockets and set off through the woods to the Save-Right. You could tell that the squirrels and birds hadn't been expecting us, because they ran up trees and screamed as soon as they heard our footsteps. For a second, I thought I saw a dead body curled on its side, but it turned out to be a log with a fine layer of moss growing over it. My heart was still pounding even after, as I rubbed the crumbly moss between my fingers, and I kicked the log to show myself how it didn't matter.

"So Knees," Jay said as we walked, "what'd your dad do when you showed him your broken arm?"

"It was awful. He looked at me like he wished I'd been an ass-posit."

My dad sometimes looked at me the same way, the one

that meant he wished he'd blown his load in my mom's butt so that I didn't exist.

Toshi squeezed his wrist, which was now freed from the cast for the day of work on New Veronia. "When he tried to look at it, I was all *ouch-ouch-ouch* so he didn't touch it too much, and plus he'd been drinking beer, so he backed off. Then, when I told him your parents paid for the whole thing, he practically cried with joy."

"Killer," I said. "Now you don't have to go to band camp?"

"He still tried to force me to go. He was so mad. He must really want the house to himself, but I told him they would probably give me another scholarship next year, plus my wrist hurt and it was impossible for me to participate and the conductor wouldn't stand for it, so I'm not going. Instead he'll just have to ignore me and take his girlfriend to a motel. I can't practice the horn, though. I'm really going to be behind when we get back to school—I bet I'll end up third chair."

The summer was starting off well—I'd come up with the idea to keep Toshi with us and his bones intact, which made me see that I might be better than I'd thought at manipulating the world.

"Have you seen the girlfriend?" Jay asked. "She hot?"

"Usually he doesn't like to bring them around. Maybe I'm too much a reminder for them that he's divorced or something."

Toshi was right about the shortcut through the woods, and we made it to the Save- Right in a bit over half an hour. Around back, stacked next to the dumpsters, were a few five-foot-high piles of pallets.

"Jackpot!" Jay shadow-boxed the air.

We each took one, hooking an arm through the slats and resting it on a shoulder, and started back towards the line of trees. The sun was higher now and sweat trickled down my spine. The bottom of my pallet kept sticking against roots and bushes, and my shoulder ached with the weight of the thing, though it had not seemed heavy at first. All this to say: I was relieved when Toshi dropped his pallet, maybe three-quarters of a mile in, and said he couldn't go any further.

"Don't be a pussy," Jay said, but he stopped and dropped his pallet, too. "We're doing fine. What's with you?"

"Maybe because I didn't eat breakfast, and plus it gave me splinters," Toshi said, which made Jay roll his eyes and say that Tosh needed to nut up.

"Yeah," I said, "nut up." Free of my pallet, I stretched my arms until the shoulder joint popped and I could feel my belly button gaping.

"Or maybe because it's hot," Toshi said. "Heat stroke is a leading cause of sudden death during exercise."

"But we have to get back, right?" I said. "Because Toshi can't do it on his own, I'll leave my pallet propped right here, and I'll help him carry his back to New Veronia, okay? And then we can come and get my pallet on the next trip."

"This is going to take fucking forever," Jay said. He hefted his pallet and began striding ahead. The side of his leg, the part that showed beneath his shorts, had three red scratches from the rough edge of the wood.

I took up the front end of Toshi's load and he took up the back. "Hold it level, won't you?" I said loud enough for Jay to hear, and with more venom than I felt. I wasn't the weak one, and I had to be sure that Jay understood that.

We trooped in silence back to the site of New Veronia. As we neared it, the brushing of my pants between my legs began to feel good, like a girl's hand cupping my balls, Stella, the girl that I would bring back to our pyramid house, and then I had an erection and I hoped feverishly that Jay wouldn't look back and see.

I'd calmed myself down by the time that we reached the huge tree that would act as the center post for our triplex. It was a beautiful old tree with marbles of sap stuck in crevices of the bark and one funny branch that crooked in the middle like an elbow. It had been there for ages, and its shade had kept much of the ground beneath it cleared of other plants.

"We'll need maybe six pallets for the floor," Jay said, "and two for each outside wall, so six more, and three more for the inside walls, that's..."

We all thought for a minute, and then Toshi said, "Fifteen pallets." He shook his head sadly. "Fifteen."

"We can get that many here in a day," Jay said. "Easy." And he started off, back through the woods. "Bennet," he said, not too loud—he knew I was right behind him. "I heard from Mark"—one of his soccer teammates—"that Stella ski poled these two guys."

The leaves all angled rightwards in a sudden breeze, their sound a flock of something alive.

Jay made Os with both of his hands and moved them up and down beside either hip, and I understood what he meant. "Like she milked them," he said.

The leaves settled, and in the calm quiet my own breathing was too audible, so I tried to pinch the air inside my nostrils. Maybe it would rain later. The sky looked clear, but the clouds could blow in and surprise you.

━━

A few hours later, the splinters in my palms looked like evil, invasive centipedes, my foot ached from where Toshi had dropped a pallet onto it, and all my skin felt lost beneath a layer of grime. We had six pallets. I felt dead tired.

Jay returned, zipping up after peeing against a tree outside of New Veronia town limits.

"Let's go," he said, "come on. We need nine more." He looked tired, too, with his mouth hanging lopsided and his eyelids swollen.

Though I wanted to help Jay, I knew that, if I didn't say something, he would keep pushing until he collapsed from exhaustion. "Maybe we should break for today? I'm starved." The packets of trail mix we'd brought had long ago been emptied, and maybe the lightheaded dullness behind my eyes was as much from hunger as it was fatigue.

"*You*," Jay said. "You people."

If I had thought that I could make it one more time back and forth from the Save-Right, if my shoulder hadn't felt dislocated from bearing the weight of all those pallets and my head shaky-light from lack of nutrients, there's no doubt that I would have kept going to make Jay happy. "We'll start again tomorrow," I said, my voice way too high. "First thing. Toshi is really beat. Right?"

"Maybe I'm getting a cold," Toshi said, too tired to defend his strength.

"Leave, then." Jay kicked at the ground and a spray of black dirt, smelling like mushrooms, rose up before him. "Go. You make me sick."

There was no doing anything with him when he was in this mood, and so I whispered to Toshi, "You ready? Let's split," and we went.

Once Toshi and I were on our bikes, I said, "Don't worry. He'll go home, too, and get some rest. He just likes to act tough or whatever."

"Sometimes," Toshi said, "I think he really hates us. But he keeps us around because we're the only ones who do what he says. Maybe we shouldn't do it. Feed right into him. Like he's a tapeworm or something, gobbling us up, getting stronger."

"You watch too much TV," I said. "He's just Jay. Our friend."

Toshi yelped; his bike swerved. He took his hands from the handlebars and massaged his temples; he must've had another headache, the worm eating his brain.

I slowed my pedaling to keep pace with him. "Chill out. Today was nothing. Probably Jay just doesn't want to go home. I mean, think about his parents. They really are sort of awful. They're always whispering to each other, like they're talking bad about everyone else. They never go to restaurants, but in the kitchen they only have frozen stuff and stuff in cans and boxes." I talked best with Toshi this way, on our bikes, the wind rushing against our faces, sort of pushing the words back in.

"I think there's something wrong with him," Toshi said, "I really do."

"You sound like a taint." Tosh must have been more upset about Jay forcing him to carry those pallets than I'd realized. "You think there's something wrong with everyone."

"But really," Toshi said, "you don't ever get the sense that Jay is…crazy, maybe?"

"No way," I said. "Or maybe we're all a little crazy. Right?"

"I saw them this one time," Toshi said, "his parents. In the gardening store, but they brushed right past without even looking at me. Maybe they don't really know who I am."

"If you think about those people, Jay came out pretty normal." I thought of Jay's parents as loners, but they were always alone *together*—maybe this made them something else. His mom was small, shorter than me, and real skinny, the wiry kind of skinny, where all the tendons stand out to make you strong looking. She had long hair she always kept back in a ponytail and she was kind of pretty, except for her buck-teeth. His dad was skinny, too, but with a tiny potbelly, and he was tall and pale, pale white, with his hair buzzed so short you couldn't see its color.

I remember the first time I saw the two of them, together of course. I was eight and they came to take Jay out of school early because they were going survivalist camping —he'd been bragging all week about purifying water and eating bugs. The whole time they waited for Jay to pack up his backpack, they were frowning. Usually when parents came to the classroom, they smiled at all us bustling students. When Jay walked over to them, they both reached out to grab one of his shoulders, and the way that their bony fingers indented his yellow-striped shirt as they guided him away has made me feel a little bit sorry for Jay ever since.

As soon as I got home, I ate practically everything in the fridge, and then I spent a long time locked in the bathroom, running fantasies through my mind. When the rain finally started, I only experienced it as a pattering on the roof above my head. *Creamed her pants. Like she milked him.* These phrases made me think of a sexy dairy farm, Stella the milkmaid in a short, blue, ruffled apron, her pretty white hands pulling at the teats of a cow.

——

The next morning, I found my dad huddled in the breakfast nook over his cup of coffee.

"How's the patio going?" he said. His voice sounded as if it hadn't been used since the last time we'd talked.

"Oh, yeah. The patio." I poured cornflakes into a bowl and added some milk and raspberries. The berries grew on a bush behind our house, and every summer I looked forward to their tart ripeness, which was more than worth the bramble scratches that tracked my arms for about three weeks running. "It's pretty okay. Jay's parents are real task masters. Work, whatever. Right?"

As I was carrying my cereal bowl to the table, to sit across from my dad, he banged a fist against the tabletop. The Santa salt and Rudolph pepper shakers—we kept the Christmas ones out all year round—jumped and clicked together. "We can't have a *conversation*," he said. "When did it start that we can't have a conversation? I remember when you were a kid, we could talk together for hours. For *hours*."

This wasn't true: I had a great memory, and neither my dad nor I had ever been big chatters. Something was off about him; normally, we comfortably ignored each other, but now he was glaring like he wanted to commit my image to memory so that he could make a voodoo doll likeness later.

"And now." He waved a hand at me disgustedly. "Not a word. Nothing to say. I don't even know you anymore. What are you up to all day, huh? What are you even thinking? You could be doing anything; I don't know. You could be plotting to blow up something."

"I'm just building a patio," I said quietly. My cornflakes were getting soggy, but if I started to eat, then I would look like a taint with milk dripping on my chin and my cheeks bulging. So that he wouldn't see past my lie, I needed to look serious. "I didn't *do* anything." I fretted that he'd somehow found out about my evening in the bathroom, the entire roll of toilet paper I'd flushed, the sad fact that I couldn't stop before my cock was red and tender and irritated.

He said, "Your little friend Toshi broke his arm. Is that right? How did that happen?"

My cheeks started to burn. "His wrist." My dad must have seen Toshi wearing that cast around the neighborhood —but he couldn't have recognized that it was my cast. Still, I worried. "It was nothing. Just an accident."

"Do you guys push him around? Was it that brute you hang out with, that… Jay?"

"No! It wasn't like that. Toshi had an accident, is all. Why; did he say something to you?"

"See, that's the kind of answer that makes me suspicious. I can't help but think about a few years ago, when that brute broke *your* wrist."

"This wasn't the same thing at all," I said. "Toshi just fell out of a tree. He lost his balance."

"Nobody pushed him? Or dared him to climb some rickety, old tree? Or had him stand somewhere with his eyes closed so that he could get pummeled?"

My dad didn't understand what had happened that day when I broke my wrist, but he'd made up his mind to blame Jay for it, even though it wasn't really Jay's fault. The three of us had snuck into the elementary school playground when it was closed for winter break. We were playing this war game, and I'd gotten my sight blown up by a grenade, so I was blindfolded and Jay was directing me around. When I was standing on the "down" end of the seesaw, a bomb blew up and hurled Jay through the air, and he landed on the seesaw's "up" end, and I was thrown into the sky, and stupidly, I stretched out my arm to break my fall.

We used to get really into these games: it was like our minds could actually build the whole make-believe world. But for some reason, that ability faded out when we got a little older. It was a matter of months that tipped us from full immersion to the double-consciousness that we looked a little silly, and soon after that, the games stopped altogether. But my dad didn't understand how in the moment, Jay had really felt that bomb hurl him through the air and plant him atop the seesaw. He hadn't meant to hurt me at all.

"Just watch out for that Toshi," my dad said. "When I was your age, me and my friends had this one guy, a younger kid, maybe a year younger than us, and we would torture him all the time. Beat him up, cut his hair, rip his homework. It was this mania with us, after a while, and so I get that you can be caught up in the frenzy…" His words faded out and his eyes stared, bleary, at nothing.

"Dad," I said, "are you going to work today? Is everything okay… at the plant?" Maybe he'd gotten demoted or something and now he was taking it out on me.

He pressed his thumbs against his temples. "This is the

reason we don't talk. You wouldn't understand. We can't understand each other." He turned away.

I started to eat my cereal, which had dissolved into the milk. If my dad had been a friend, I would have told him to snap out of it, or to muzzle up, or to go get laid and muzzle up, but he wasn't a friend, so I ate and finished eating and put my bowl in the sink.

———

When Toshi and I biked to the edge of the woods and then walked the shrubby stretch into New Veronia, we found fifteen pallets stacked up beside the center post tree.

"Fifteen." Toshi counted them twice. "Fifteen. He must have worked all night. He probably broke his back doing it."

Not until then did I noticed a navy blue smudge on the brown and green ground. The navy blue was Jay's shirt, and Jay was in it, sleeping.

"Let him rest," I said. "He walked back and forth eighteen times for those other pallets."

"And they were heavy, too," Toshi said, "you felt how they were heavy."

This was the reason we looked up to Jay, the reason he was our leader: he got shit done.

For a while, we messed around rearranging things, some hammers, a couple saws, plenty of nails, all stuff borrowed from our homes, but it was hard to get anything done without Jay directing us, so when he uncurled from the fetal position and opened his eyes, I felt relieved.

"You really got nine pallets after we left?" I said. "Nine!"

Jay's shorts were torn, a pink scratch angled across his cheek, and a couple twigs were stuck to his forehead.

"Tell me if you feel like you're dying," Toshi said, looking truly concerned. "People can over-exhaust themselves and then just keel over. You watch Bennet and me today. We'll do the hard stuff."

"No, man." Jay stretched and brushed away the twigs. "I feel fine. I'll help."

A rush of love for Jay overwhelmed me then. We'd done everything together: biked tens of miles, all the way into Maryland, to buy cigarettes from this gas station we'd heard didn't card (but they did card, and so we never got the Marlboros); played this weird game when we were kids that was all about making up new words for everyday things, and at the same time, reading each other's minds; we'd gotten drunk for the first time together and still did whenever we could get our hands on anything. I knew that he'd worked like crazy just to bring us enough wood to build New Veronia. Jay and I would always be best friends. I handed him a granola bar that was still warm from my pocket, and he ate it in one bite, then declared that we needed to start constructing the outside walls.

"Measure twice, cut once!" Jay kept shouting happily. For passing out on the ground, getting bitten by bugs all night, he seemed chipper.

The huge trees kept rustling in a high-up breeze that didn't reach us down there on the forest floor. When I overturned a rock, weird red insects with wings flew up against my face; they didn't sting, but brushed softly and fluttered off. Because we were working in the open air, we smelled not our sweat, but the sweetish pollen of blooming things and the dry sawdust and dirt—unless we got too close to the north side of New Veronia, where the bear trap stank like rotting horseshoe crabs.

I'd never really built anything before. Once, my dad had bought me a wooden model of a T-Rex skeleton, but that had been on such a small scale, and it came with detailed directions. This project, our New Veronia, was from scratch, which made it feel all the more important. And when we were finished, we'd have our own little city, a place where we could be kings, where we could do basically whatever we wanted—Jay would tell us what that was.

After we had been at work for a few hours, we all collapsed with our backs to the same stunted black walnut and shared the peanut butter and jelly sandwiches that Toshi had brought. I contributed a quart of Coke and a package of Oreos. We grabbed for the cookies at the same time, and there was something harmonious about our hands all there with their matching scratches and bruised knuckles and splinters. We were in this together, all working hard on the biggest project we'd ever taken on.

As soon as lunch was reduced to a pile of empty wrappers, Jay wanted to get straight back to it.

"At this rate," I said, "we'll have the whole thing finished in no time!"

"Then we won't have anything to do the rest of summer." Toshi held up the tape measurer. "And the boredom will kill us." But he started to pencil measurements onto the wood; I could tell that he was secretly happy, now that he knew he didn't need to haul pallets all day.

"Another eight feet," Jay said, "eight feet exactly. You know Stephanie? Stephanie... Heller?"

"You mean Helmet," Toshi said. The tape measurer connected him and Jay as they marked out the eight feet. "That's what they call her: Stephanie Helmet. Because she uses so much hair spray, makes her hair all hard like a big helmet on her head."

"Whatever, Tosh, we get it," I said. Ready with the saw, I felt impatient to start my cutting. The back and forth motion, the way the saw buzzed softly in my hand as it bit through the wood, the snap when the one piece became two—it all made me feel *good*.

"Hairspray is sexy," Jay said. "The way it smells on a woman."

"But when you *touch* it, all sticky…"

"Toshi, come on. When have you ever touched a woman?"

I laughed hard until I remembered that Jay could have said the exact same thing to me. Still, that was the whole point of New Veronia.

"Hairspray makes her hair feel sort of hard, yeah, but not sticky. It's dry, I mean the stuff dries on their hair like that." Jay finally lowered his pencil to the wood and marked the spot. When he stood, he adjusted himself inside his shorts. "It makes their hair feel… sort of like a statue's hair. How it's carved out of marble like that, but you can still see the strands. And you know all those statues, those sexy statues…?"

Jay didn't have to explain any more. In the fifth grade, we'd all three of us gone on a field trip to the art museum up in Philadelphia, and the pictures were pretty good with the naked ladies in color, but the best things were the three dimensional nudes carved out of white stone. You could circle those bodies again and again, looking from all different angles. We talked about those statues incessantly for weeks, and here we were, all these years later, still talking about them.

"We met up after school one day," Jay said. "Steph wanted me to help her with her homework. I know, you're laughing. Of course right then I knew it was a setup. So we met and we went back to her place—her dad was home, but I guess he never leaves his basement office—and her room had this frilly pink bed and pink all over the walls, *stuffed animals*, even, a teddy bear, like bears are for cuddling, god girls are so stupid, and I sat down on the bed and she sat down next to me."

I wondered why I hadn't heard this story before, when it had first happened, for example. Maybe Jay was lying, or maybe he'd been saving this story up so that he could shock me and Toshi. Jay had stopped working; he stood next to our pile of pallets, the tape measurer he held in one hand smacking rhythmically against the other palm. Toshi and I were still crouched down by the piece of wood we were about to cut, and I rocked back onto my bottom since my thighs were burning.

Jay said, "She sat with a foot up on the bed and a foot on the ground so that her skirt sort of hiked up one thigh. She knew what she was up to. She knew. She wiggled until our legs were touching along the side and then she started kissing me."

"Just like that?" Toshi asked. I could see that he was really into the story: he picked up a saw so that he could hold it in front of his pants. All this I caught from the corner of my eye—it couldn't look like I'd been looking.

"Pretty soon—I couldn't believe it, but it's true—Steph crawled right up into my lap. She might have let me do it to her, too, but then her mom came home and we had to stop."

I realized that I'd been holding my breath. I let it out in a whoosh and asked when all this had happened.

"Right before finals. I'm sure neither one of us did so good in geography or whatever it was we were supposed to be studying. But her hair, man, it felt so perfect. Every strand carved out."

Tosh was sort of half-collapsed over sitting there on the ground. Hoping that I didn't look all smooshed the way Toshi did, I stood up. "Well," I said, "during finals week, I was in a study group with Allison. The blond."

"You mean Allison Ruiz? That's dyed, man," Jay said.

"Still looks good," Toshi murmured into his knees.

"We were doing math, I think, but I wasn't paying attention because she had on this top that was cut down to...." I drew a line between my nipples with my pointer finger. My story was fake, but the shirt was an actual shirt I'd seen on Stella the week before. A sky blue shirt that brought out the color of her eyes. "I love how she smells like caramel."

Jay shook his head. "All these girls are always wearing that candy perfume shit. I wish I could smell how they really are. Their dirty parts and everything."

"Yeah," I said, worried that this was yet another sign of how much less a man I was than Jay, that I wanted sugar and he wanted authentic. "I mean, me too."

Jay said, "How about Allison's mom? She don't even look old. I mean, I would do her."

"Doesn't," Toshi corrected. His favorite subject was English, which I sometimes thought strange because he was the only one of us who looked like English might not be his first language, which it was. Apparently, even in Singapore, where his mom was from, but where he'd never been, everyone spoke English. "Do you think Allison will come to New Veronia with you?" Toshi asked me. "When it's finished."

His question made me feel awful; Allison Ruiz wasn't a real person to me, just like I wasn't one to her. The most interaction we'd had was avoiding bumping into each other in the hallways at school. "Let's get back to work," I said as I reached over and took my saw from Toshi.

He looked down at his empty hands and then turned them over, palms down. "There was this girl in the Dover Downs," he said, "when I was there with my dad. We saw each other in the crowd. She came right over to me."

"And?" Jay asked. "*And?*"

"I don't kiss and tell. I protect a woman's honor."

"Seriously?" Jay groaned and I could tell that his imagination was making up all kinds of awesome sex acts between Toshi and the casino girl. "Come on, Knees, you only got to *honor* a wife. Like my dad, he thinks my mom is a goddess—he calls her that, even—but all the women he did before her are just trash. No need for loyalty to trash."

Toshi mimed zipping up his lips and tossing away the key. He was so smart that way: whatever Jay and I imagined was definitely crazier than what had really happened.

If only I had embellished *my* story more, made it so that I at least got to feel up one of Allison's breasts, instead of just looking at them. Then it would be me getting interrogated by Jay. Because Jay was magnetic, always upbeat, and it was like you wanted as much of his attention as you could get, to feed into his energy.

▭

After we worked for a couple more hours, Jay said we should take a break and have some fun. While Toshi and I tidied up around New Veronia, he walked to his house to grab a shotgun and a bag full of empty beer bottles.

"Target practice," he said, grinning, when he broke back into the clearing. He had the gun slung over one shoulder, hip cocked out; the goatee glinted on his chin.

We walked maybe half a mile deeper into the woods, and then Jay went first: I threw the bottles up high as I could while he aimed and fired. Half the time, the bottle shattered against the ground, but the other half, he blasted it apart in midair, the glass transforming into a galaxy of shards that hung in the sky for an instant before they fell away to nothing.

"Who wants to go next?" Jay said. "Knees?"

Toshi shook his head. "An average of twenty-nine people die from gunshots every day."

"Why you always spouting off these stupid numbers?" Jay said. Toshi just shrugged, but I knew why: it was because the statistics were irrefutable facts, things Jay couldn't argue with. This little part of Tosh was preserved and separate from us, but he had to show it off sometimes so that we'd remember it was there. The statistics were Toshi's armor.

"What's wrong," Jay said, "your dad never teach you to shoot? Maybe afraid you'd end up on the wrong side of a war?" Jay raised the shotgun to his shoulder and swung the barrel around until it was pointed straight at Toshi. The skin on my scalp shrunk up closer to the bone as the sunlight fell over us in waves.

"My grandpa fought in the forties," Jay said, "right after Pearl Harbor."

"Put it down," I said. Jay's finger was on the trigger, and I knew he wouldn't do anything crazy, but I also knew that he was unpredictable and that any little thing could leave him livid. My muscles felt watery, but they were still able to move me away from Toshi, out of the gun's sight.

"They wouldn't have trusted any of you then," Jay said to Toshi. "During the war."

The broken glass, amber and green, glittered around us. I wanted to tell Toshi to run, but that would have been acknowledging that the situation was more than a joke, and if I pretended hard enough that it was all a put-on, maybe it would be.

"And now we welcome you into this country," Jay said. "Isn't that weird?"

Toshi nodded slowly. Somehow, he was holding it together; he didn't even look scared; his face was an emotionless mask. He licked his lower lip and squinted against the sun.

Jay said, "I always wondered about what could happen if I didn't shoot at the target." He pulled in a noisy breath and said, "Pa-chow!" My stomach jumped without me.

Then Jay let the shotgun fall to his side, and he started to laugh, and Toshi and I joined in, all of us laughing way too hard.

Later, when Toshi and I were biking back to our neighborhood, I said, "You didn't really do anything with that girl at the casino, did you?"

Toshi stared at me with big, lying eyes. "How did you know?" he said. "I mean, how would you know? You've never gotten a girl's attention. Jay said so; we all know it. And I *did*. I did."

"What do you mean, *Jay said so?*" I veered my bike away from his, taking a sharp left where we always went straight. I couldn't believe that Jay was talking with Toshi about me behind my back. When Jay had pointed that gun at Tosh—I know this thought was stupid—but when he did that, it was like he was giving Toshi special attention.

I pedaled hard so that my thighs burned with the effort, and when a car zipped by in the other direction, the speed of it nearly blew me off course. But even though I was biking faster than I'd ever biked before, when I checked over my shoulder, Toshi was right behind me.

"What is your problem?" Toshi said. "I mean, no big deal. In New Veronia, you'll touch some girl's ass soon."

Winded, I couldn't answer; I slowed my pace and scooted rightward so that Toshi and I could bike side-by-side in one lane.

When I caught my breath, I said, "I'm just sick of you two lying. I don't want to have to lie, just to fit in."

"You think Jay made up all that stuff about Stephanie Helmet?"

"Maybe. I don't know. Yeah, some of it." Between each sentence, I panted.

"Well, I don't. I've heard rumors about her. Her name is scratched in the last stall of the bathroom in the cafeteria."

"That doesn't mean anything. Jay might have done that himself, to make what he said seem more real."

A car came up behind us and honked. We pulled closer to the shoulder, which was the width of a piece of paper and dropped off into a ditch, like the shoulders of most all the roads that ran between neighborhoods in Delaware, one lane each way, nothing but the double-yellow lines to separate the cars.

My heart wouldn't slow down, and I was tired out from all the angry biking, so I pulled over into the parking lot of a little roadside liquor store. Jay and I had once tried to get a man to buy us beer from this store, but instead the guy had pocketed our money and ducked out the back. Toshi had never seemed much interested in drinking, which made me glad, because it was one thing Jay and I could do together, without him.

Toshi and I pulled our bikes around the side and sat on the curb. I sort of wanted to be left alone, but I also felt glad for Toshi's company. Because it was summer, the sun wouldn't set for hours. It pressed down on my shoulders and made everything feel wet, like a teabag just pulled from a steaming cup.

"My mother is dead," I said. She used to drink chamomile tea, and she always steeped each teabag twice. There would be one waiting for her on a saucer beside the sink.

"Oh, no," Toshi said, "when did you find out? Who told you?"

A line of ants marched between my sneakers and then disappeared down a crack in the pavement. I lifted a foot and brought it down on the line. When I moved my foot back, the live ones kept marching, veering around their dead coworkers. "No one told me," I said. "I just know it." One ant palpitated the squished body of another with his antennae, but then he moved on without taking further action. "Sometimes I feel like I fell off a stool, a really high stool, onto a concrete floor, and I hit my head really hard and now everything is just a little bit off."

Toshi stared at me before he said, "*Did* you hit your

head? It happens all the time, and you could get a concussion and die without even realizing it."

It was so hard for us to understand each other; maybe impossible. I shrugged.

"So your mom isn't really dead."

"The shitty thing is that she *could* be and I wouldn't even know."

Toshi reached out and put his hand on my knee, but only for a second; he must have realized that it looked gay. He said, "That's true about my mom, too. At least, it would probably take a week before someone thought to tell me."

"Yeah."

A pickup that looked exactly like my dad's pulled in and parked crookedly, and then my dad got out of it.

"He should still be at the plant." I tried to make myself small so that he wouldn't notice me. My dad beelined for the entrance. "He must have got off a little early."

"Oh no"—Toshi held out his naked wrist—"my cast."

I helped him put it on. Bits of old plaster rubbed off onto my thumbs, and the athletic tape was losing its stick. "Don't worry; my dad didn't see us. Do you wear it in the shower? You'll need to replace this tape soon."

"Now I do. One time I left it on the bathroom counter beside the soap dispenser and my dad came in to pee, but luckily, he didn't notice it. Probably it's him making me sick all the time: he never washes his hands."

"That's good," I said.

Chapter 4

In the morning, I headed over to the site as soon as I woke up, a granola bar stuffed into my pocket. I was early: not even Jay was there yet. We'd marked out the positions for the doors the day before, and I started furiously cutting along the penciled lines, the saw rattling the bones inside my arm. I felt cold, though the morning chill had already lifted.

The night before, I'd had an old dream, one I'd used to have as a kid: I was locked in a box with one little hole I could peek out of, and through it I could see people on a bed, but no matter how loudly I called out to them, they didn't seem to notice me. I would suffocate in that box; I would starve. In the dream, one by one, my ribs started to show beneath my skin.

"Hey."

Jay was standing over me; I hadn't even heard him approach. Maybe something was wrong with my ears. I stuck a finger inside one and dug out a turd of wax, then wiped vigorously at my face before looking up. Even the memory of the dream had shaken me.

"You're awake early," he said, and the fact that he didn't

ask me what was wrong reminded me what a good friend he was: he knew when to give me space.

Jay watched me for a minute more and then said that he'd seen a house where they were remodeling, not far from my neighborhood, and they had taken all the old doors off and left them in a pile beside a dumpster—free, if we could get to them first.

"We'll go over there today," he said. "Now."

"Shouldn't we wait for Toshi?"

"Naw. I don't see why. Nut up."

And when I thought about Toshi arriving in New Veronia, finding it empty, then realizing that Jay and I must be off somewhere together, I felt a mean twinge of happiness.

As we started walking back through the woods, Jay seemed to read my mind: he said, "Sometimes I feel like Toshi just doesn't get us."

I said carefully, "I mean, he's not as fun as you."

"Maybe it's because he's mixed. Like that mixes you up." He grabbed a pebble and chucked it at a squirrel. The pebble clattered against a tree as the squirrel's tail flicked us off before disappearing among the leaves.

Jay's garage was filled with junk: chains snaked across the floor, several gun racks held one or two pieces each, boxes overflowed with plastic stuff. There were empty cartons, broken old lawnmowers, a pile of sticks, a flat of Coke with half the cans gone.... No room for a car. Jay walked over to one corner and began pushing aside a collection of old magazines until he uncovered his bicycle.

"Tires seem okay," he said, testing them. He picked up a rope from the cracked concrete floor and overturned a kiddie pool, underneath of which sat a little red wagon. "We'll use this to tie the doors onto and pull them back. Okay?"

"Nice," I said.

"I been thinking"—Jay started tying the wagon onto his bike—"it might be about time that we replace Toshi. We're getting older, and he's not like us. It's just, I don't want the guys asking weird questions. Soccer starts up again soon."

"Yeah." I wasn't exactly sure what Jay was ranting about, but it seemed like he was saying I was his favorite, and Toshi was far behind me. Tosh had always been the dorkiest of us, with his slightly-off clothes and his dedication to the school band.

Jay said, "When you think about it, Toshi shouldn't even be here. Like his mom? She probably married Toshi's dad just so that she could be a US citizen."

"Then how come she went back to Singapore?" I said.

"It might be that Knees isn't our kind of guy, I mean, we'll be *sophomores* soon. We got to make sure they know what sort of men we are."

"He should have gone with her," I said. "To Singapore." Sometimes I wondered what my life would've been like if, after the divorce, I'd gone to live with my mom instead of my dad.

"Yeah. He would've been better off there. He belongs there, really."

Jay's reasoning wasn't quite my reasoning, but if we wound up at the same conclusion, the route didn't seem to matter much.

Jay and I pedaled down the road with the wagon tied to Jay's bike. He wobbled a little bit at first—I couldn't remember the last time I'd seen him ride—but soon he righted himself and was fine, though he had a gawky, bandy-kneed way of coasting. We passed the house, field, field, house, field, field, field that was the makeup of Jay's neighborhood. You could tell which fields had been recently tilled from the vultures suspended above them; the birds were searching for the littered bodies of mice and rabbits. When we reached the house, the free doors were still there.

"They're really just giving these away?" I asked. The

pressed wood looked real enough, and they had little glass windows across their tops.

"Yeah, come on, Bennet, lend a hand." Jay was strapping the doors down tight on the little red wagon.

"These doors already have windows in them, so maybe we won't need to cut out holes for windows, too. That shit takes a long time. Doors and windows in one!"

"Works for me," Jay said.

The ride back to New Veronia was slow, with Jay and me switching off turns pedaling the bike hauling the door-stacked wagon. Cars kept honking at us because Jay had tied the doors on long-ways, so they stuck out pretty far into the lane, and at one point, we had a line of maybe seven cars inching along behind us.

"Impatient fuckers!" Jay would yell at a car when it whizzed by too close to our doors.

———

Back at New Veronia, we found Toshi sitting against a tree. "You're not even working," I said. "What good are you?"

"I've been waiting here all morning." Toshi stood up, but his foot must have fallen asleep, because he sort of lurched on it. "I've been doing stuff, I cut a window hole, but then this bug bit me. It hurts a lot." He held out a finger, but I didn't see any bug bite. "Where have you been? I mean, what have you been doing?"

"A *window* hole?" I said, and Jay echoed me. I saw where Toshi had done it: in just one of the walls, thank god.

Jay said, "We've nixed the windows. No more windows. That wall with the hole in it can be yours. Sure, you can have a hole to let the cold in and invite everyone spying on you."

"What do you mean, we're not doing windows? They were part of the plan."

"We got these doors." Jay slapped a palm against them.

"Windows right here in the doors, and high enough up no one can see what's going on inside the room. Privacy, right—that's what we need. Plus, windows are a weakness—a spot where the bears could get in."

We worked in a huffy silence until just after noon, when Jay said he had to go do something with his parents, so I started for home. Toshi stayed behind in New Veronia. I worried that he was mad at me before I remembered that, even if he was, I shouldn't care: I was above him in the hierarchy, the one who belonged at Jay's side.

When I passed the front of Jay's house, I found Stella sunbathing in a purple bikini. Her eyes were closed, and I got off my bike and stood there for about five minutes, arguing with myself, before I threw my shoulders back and walked up to her.

"Nice day out," I said. "Summer, I mean." I worked to make my voice buzz against my throat, which edited it down to a nice baritone.

She slowly opened her eyes and turned her head towards me. "Sure." She picked up the book that was tented over her stomach.

Her hair was loose—it was rarely loose—and the sunlight made it glitter. I wanted to ask her to sit on my lap, but of course I couldn't. Since she had entered high school, or before that, even, when everything between girls and boys had started to become sexual, we hadn't really talked to each other, but I thought about her so often it was like we were married. I felt tied to her by my soul, a connection that I knew was real because of the mini heart attack I suffered each time I saw her, and the fact that, despite my pain, I always seemed more alive afterward. "What are you reading?"

"*Handmaid's Tale.*" Her eyebrows lowered beneath her dark glasses.

"I haven't read that one. Sounds killer." Standing above

her made me feel awkward, but I also had a great vantage of her boobs and stomach and legs.

"It's about how men ruin women," she said.

"Okay." I'd been thinking about her body too much; I was afraid she might notice. "Well, I better get going. Hey, you're signed up for AP history, right?" I'd worked hard and petitioned the school to be allowed into this class because I knew that Stella would be taking it.

"Yeah." She raised her book up above the level of her eyes.

⸻

After breaking ground on New Veronia, I don't know how much the others were masturbating, by my rate doubled. I'd read about the sperm building up inside you, how some native tribes used to use that excess of swimmers battling within your body to increase your warfighting power, but letting it all out seemed to make me more productive. If I didn't jerk off, all I could think about was jerking off, but if I just beat it, then I could focus on something else until the urge overtook me again. Because my father was home even less than usual, I had plenty of time and privacy to pursue this preoccupation.

That triangle of purple fabric stretched above Stella's thighs became an immediate new obsession: I would visualize it until it began to expand and contract and change from purple to blue to gold. That bottom half of bikini was like one of those 3D posters that morphed into something amazing after you stared at it for a while.

⸻

Over the next several weeks, Jay and Toshi and I worked tirelessly on New Veronia. It was like we all three got tunnel vision: we patched up gaps in the floors and the walls, we pieced them all together into a pyramid and then nailed all the pieces to each other and the central tree post, we draped tarps over the roof. Toshi brought over some sealant that his dad had used to waterproof someone's gazebo, and we went over the outside of our structure. We hung the doors. Toshi covered up the window cutout on his side with plywood. I was amazed at how nice the whole thing looked, and it held together pretty well, too. Sure, there were a fair amount of gaps, and doors that didn't shut well, and places that squeaked when you stepped on them, and nails poking out at odd angles, and you could stub a toe on a floorboard if you weren't careful, but overall, I didn't fear that the whole thing would tumble down around me in a big gust of wind.

On the morning that we were supposed to build the outhouse, Jay didn't show, so we decided to look for him at his house. Maybe he'd slept in.

Toshi and I walked through the front door without knocking—Jay's parents would be at work, and I always hoped that maybe Stella would be lounging in her underwear and I'd surprise her—only what we found was a weird séance: the whole family was seated around the coffee table, Jay's mom and dad on the couch, sitting close together as if for warmth, with Jay and Stella cross-legged on the floor opposite them.

Jay's mom looked stoic, except for her hands: they were smoothing over each other, pulling at fingers, twitching as if jerked by some force not a part of her body. A bunch of stuff was stacked up on the coffee table, albums and loose pictures, and there was a pile of what looked and smelled like home-made muffins, though I'd never seen that kind of food before in Jay's house.

"Sorry," I said automatically as the whole family looked up at our intrusion.

Jay's mom had red eyes, and she quickly began to scoop all the pictures into a cardboard box.

"It's okay," Stella said. "We were done anyway." She flounced away towards the stairs and my heart, trembling, followed her.

Without Stella, the room grew spooky and quiet, and I wanted to leave, but since Jay was still sitting on the floor, staring into his lap, that seemed ruder than just awkwardly waiting around.

"Remember what we talked about, son," Jay's father said to him, and I was struck by the kindness in his tone, the civility of the sentence. My dad had never spoken to me that way. "Hunting is a way of life. Could be a model for life, too. In the crosshairs. On the wrong track. All those things mean something in hunting, and they mean something in life." Jay's dad watched as Jay's mom carried the albums out of the room. "The kill matters. You come home empty-handed, you got nothing to show. The kill matters; it's our way of life."

Jay nodded, his expression flat and determined.

Finally Jay's dad stood up. He hadn't looked at us the whole time, which felt like a brush-off. He said, "You demand respect for yourself, son, is the only way you'll get it."

After Jay's parents had left (for work, I assumed) our threesome made the way to New Veronia.

Toshi walked right beside Jay, kind of leaving me behind, and I heard him say, "I forgot today was his birthday. Are you going to be okay?"

"Fuck off," Jay said loudly. "I don't care about that shit. We just did it for my mom."

Toshi kicked a rock that skittered through the underbrush like something alive. I hated it when I was left out this way, and I wanted to ask them what they were talking about, but I knew from the affront of their backs that they weren't ready to tell me.

When we reached New Veronia, I said, "It's impressive. "I mean, if you were a girl, wouldn't you be impressed?"

Each of the three walls was maybe ten feet long, and they sloped up sharply against the tree. The varnished wood shone in the sunlight, and the blue tarps looked sort of like the topping on a cake.

"Yeah," Toshi said, "it's lopsided, but my town looks pretty good."

"Your town?" Jay sneered. "This is *my* town." Jay's tone reminded me how he'd talked about cutting off Toshi from our friend group—maybe he'd get mad enough to really do it. A sort of dreadful excitement fingered my guts.

"It belongs to all of us," Toshi said. "We all thought up parts of it."

"What are you, a commie?" Jay pushed Tosh in the chest and he stumbled back slightly. "It was *my* idea."

I started to cut in to confirm that Jay had the idea first, but then I thought better of it: I didn't want Jay to notice me, to turn his anger my way.

"Everyone is always trying to steal everything from me," Jay said. "Like they don't think I'm good enough to have it. But you're not taking this, Knees; no fucking way." Jay stepped close to Toshi and grabbed his arm, the one that was supposed to be broken, with both hands. When Toshi tried to wrench away, Jay held tighter, his grip draining Toshi's skin to white. "Check out this pussy," Jay said to me.

If I agreed, it would put me firmly on Jay's side, the two of us against an enemy, but it also might pump up Jay enough to start beating on Tosh.

"There's enough wood," I said loudly and gestured at the pile of it. My tactic: distraction. "We have leftovers. For a privacy screen around the toilet. That will be important. Right?"

Jay looked at me, his eyes still hard and angry, but then he nodded and his face softened. Sometimes he could do that, just let go, but other times he would grab on and shake like a pit bull with a Chihuahua.

Himself again, Jay walked over to the extra wood and started lining it up. "The girls probably won't even want us to know that they go to the bathroom," Jay said. "We can make a real big privacy screen. It's hilarious, right, because they have three holes down there"—he circled a hand around his groin—"and I plan to fuck in all of them."

"Three holes?" Toshi said. He was going to drop it, too, but then, he always did.

"Butthole. Piss hole. Coochie hole." Jay let his fingers pop up—one, two, three—as he spoke.

"I'm pretty sure you can't do it in the pee hole," I said. "It's too small."

"Aren't the pee hole and the coochie hole the same?" Toshi asked.

Jay stopped straightening up the leftover wood. "You two ass-posits. Just wait until you get some girls over here. Then you can see for yourselves."

I grinned hard at the ground—we were all a big, happy family again, just like that.

"You think that we're almost ready for the girls to come over?" Toshi asked.

"What I'm thinking about," Jay said, "is mattresses. No woman is going to want to have sex on a wood floor, get splinters in her ass, whatever. We need some nice, big mattresses to get them in the mood."

We all thought about Tony's Mattress Madness then, which was this mattress store out on One that always had a pile of almost brand-new mattresses in its dumpster. My dad had gotten me a dumpster mattress a few years ago, and you couldn't tell the difference. You really couldn't.

"Tony's," Jay said.

Toshi looked worried. "Tony's is miles away," he said.

"Miles and miles. We can't drag them back here. I'll pop a disc."

"I have an idea about that." Jay had a secret; we could tell from the curl of his lip, the same look that meant he'd stolen a fifth of Southern Comfort or figured out how to head butt the soccer ball perfectly every single time. "We'll just use my dad's truck."

I shook my head. "It will look suspicious. If we pile three king-sized into the back of your dad's truck, won't he wonder what we're doing?" I was also worried about being in a cab with Jay's dad, who would probably sit there in stony, uncomfortable silence, or maybe get mad that my head was blocking the side view mirror and clock me with his fist.

"The thing is," Jay said, "*I* can drive. My dad will never know."

Chapter 5

We had to do the heist at night, of course. Jay said his father would kill him if he found out about the truck, and there were signs posted all over Tony's dumpsters that said Private Property, No Trespassing, Trespassers Will Be Prosecuted, et cetera. At midnight, I left the house under cover of darkness, but out the front door, since my dad hadn't come home yet. Toshi and I met on the street. Our neighborhood looked better in the dark, which softened the crab grass and gave it the illusion of lush green carpet.

"You have trouble getting out?" I asked him.

"My dad fell asleep on the couch," he said, "but I was super quiet. I hate staying up this late. I'll have a headache all tomorrow."

"Come on, let's get going. We got to meet Jay in twenty." I tried to sound important, like I knew what I was doing, though I felt scared.

Together we walked to a spot about halfway between our houses and Jay's, where no one lived and likely no one would see Jay pick us up.

"To the cross," Toshi said. "We're meeting him at the cross?"

"Yeah."

The only marker on this long, dark stretch of road lined with trees and soybean fields was a white-painted cross someone had put up for a kid who'd been run over by a car. There wasn't a name or any dates, just the two pieces of wood nailed together.

"Here comes Jay," I said at the first rumble of an engine. "Pull your ski mask on, okay?"

Jay parked precisely beside us, and before we climbed into the cab with him, I saw that he'd smeared mud over the license plate. "Jay," I said, "where'd you learn to drive?"

"My dad taught me. Obviously. When is yours going to?"

I said, "Maybe I'll have to be self-taught."

"Better not." Jay flicked the truck into a smooth forward roll. "You might ruin the gears that way. I could show you, though. It's not too hard. At least, it wasn't for me."

Toshi said, "Your dad taught you even though you don't have a learner's permit?"

Headlights were coming at us, and I worried about those double-yellow lines, the only barrier between us and the other car.

Jay said, "What if he and Ma need a trip to the hospital? Family comes first, and I got to pull my weight. Or what if there's a war?"

When the headlights zipped past us without incident, my body still jolted as if there had been a collision. Toshi's widened eyes, highlighted by the ski mask, looked ghostly, floating there without a face.

"What if the government tries to take over, and it's the apocalypse, and I have to escape? You never know what might happen. Driving a car is just one of those skills you need. Don't matter your age."

"Your age doesn't matter," Toshi said, quietly.

We reached Tony's Mattress Madness at about one in the morning. A single orange light glowed in the parking lot, but when we pulled around to the back, where the dumpsters lived, all was black. We looked at each other in our ski masks, our eyes disconnected, no more than strange, gelatinous slits floating in the dark.

The bright-white mattresses glowed faintly, and I wondered if they were the source of the eggy smell that hung in the air.

"Are there security cameras?" Toshi asked.

"If there are, now they have your voice."

Toshi clapped his hands over his mouth, and Jay laughed at him.

We blew past all of the No Trespassing and Beware signs and walked straight over to the mattresses, which were piled up like a messy stack of pancakes.

"Grab the hugest ones," Jay said. The ski mask made his body look bigger, or maybe just his head look smaller.

"And the cleanest. For the girls. That's what the girls will want."

As we heaved the soft and surprisingly heavy things into the back of the truck, I kept expecting a police siren to sound or a floodlight to illuminate this illegal thing that we were doing, but we loaded three queens without incident. After Jay had slammed the tailgate, he grabbed something out of the cab that rattled in his hand. I didn't realize what it was until after he'd spray-painted the first penis over the Beware sign.

"You do one," Jay said and handed me the can.

"I don't really want to," I said. "How do you even get the shape right?"

"Nut up," Jay said.

It wasn't like he'd tried to convince me or threatened me or ridiculed me, it was just that I'd always done what he'd said. I was *compelled* to do it. I took the can; it felt lighter than I'd expected. I shook it and then sprayed.

"That's great, Bennet." Jay slapped me on my back. "See? A black dick. That's what Tony the mattress man has."

I grinned and handed back the can.

As Toshi and I tied down the mattresses, Jay sprayed some more, and when I looked back, I saw that he'd drawn two more penises and connected them into a swastika.

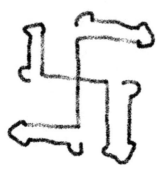

"Holy shit," he said, "check out that work of art."

The wind threw up dust and shoved the sulfur smell of the dumpsters against my nose, and I looked away from the graffiti as my stomach walloped the inside of my spine.

As we rode home, Toshi kept saying, "Wow." He sat in the middle of the bench seat, between me and Jay. The bitch seat. "Wow, wow, wow. We did it."

He didn't sound so much happy as shocked.

"Probably we're going to get caught," he said. "They could always pick us up later." He pulled off his ski mask, then Jay and I did the same. My hair, buzzed with electricity, prickled skywards from my scalp.

When we reached the edge of the woods, Jay finagled the truck through a narrow path almost the whole way to New Veronia. We unloaded and propped the mattresses against some trees. The plan was for me and Toshi to stand watch over our loot while Jay returned the truck. His father, he said, would never know.

"See?" Jay stuck his head out of the driver's window right

before he pulled away. The bumper sticker of an American flag glowed red in the brake lights. "A real man does stuff with a truck."

THESE COLORS......
DON'T RUN

Something about the half-sneer on his face, the cocky tilt of his elbow out the window, made me remembered the pallets and how Jay had gotten nine of them, somehow, overnight, when it had taken the three of us all day to get six. How did I not see before that it would have been impossible for Jay to carry those nine pallets for mile after mile through the woods in the dark? We'd found him the next day curled up in New Veronia, but he hadn't acted tired. He must've used his father's truck to get the pallets, and then let us think that he'd done all that work by hand, let us think he was superhuman, almost.

When Jay returned after parking the truck, he acted completely normal—but he had no reason not to. He hadn't really lied, because he'd never said how he'd gotten the pallets, and we'd never asked. Jay heaved up one end of a mattress and I held the other and we carried it off, Toshi following behind and not really contributing much of anything.

"Jay," I said, "did you ever think of using the truck as a place to get with girls?"

"Couldn't do that," he said. "My dad would strangle me.

It's not about keeping his upholstery clean or whatever. He said if Ma ever smelled pootang in there, she'd think he was messing around on her, and she'd kill him."

"Huh," I said. Jay's parents were one of the few married couples I knew anything about, but still I felt pretty sure that they were strange. I wanted to ask him about that morning, about the pictures on the coffee table, but even though it seemed like a simple question, of course it wasn't, not with Jay.

He said, "I saw this show about this bear that broke into a guy's truck. He hit the gear shift with his paw, and the truck started rolling backwards down this hill…"

Chapter 6

We spent the last day of summer vacation hanging out in New Veronia. When Jay was dribbling his soccer ball, Toshi was playing his horn (in New Veronia, he could free himself of the fake cast and practice, his trills and toots scattering the birds and disturbing the wood's stillness), and I was reading the play we were putting on in theater that upcoming semester, a shout echoed off the trees.

"Boys?" the voice said. It was my dad's. "Boys, you back here?"

The three of us froze and then glanced at each other. The afternoon had almost become evening, and the squirrel we'd named Dave was busily running up and down the trunk of his favorite tree.

"Dad?" I said, when he finally lurched into the clearing.

"Well," he said, "this is the strangest looking patio I have ever seen."

His eyes were bloodshot and his voice had that twangy, blurred quality that meant he'd downed too many. Toshi and Jay and I were standing in different parts of the New Veronia clearing, but as my dad moved closer to us, we grouped together between him and the house. Toshi kept his arm behind his back, hiding the fact that he wasn't wearing the cast. My dad stopped about six feet from us and stared up at the structure.

"What a piece of crap," he said. "I never seen anything that looked so junky."

"It's just a fort," I said. I thought I could smell his sweet-rotten alcohol breath, but it might have been all the decomposing stuff in the woods.

"Looks like a junky bunker in a third world country." He swayed on his feet.

"Pretty sure you ain't never served," Jay said, "so what would you know about bunkers?"

As my dad worked to focus his eyes on Jay, a deep and burning humiliation pulsed through my guts. "Son," he said to Jay, "I never liked you. I don't know you, but I don't like you."

"Dad," I said, my insides roiling, "please get out of here."

"You lied to me," he said. "There's no patio on that piece of crap house. The girl told me you all disappear back here every day, though."

Stella had seen my father this way: the injustice of it all burned at my eyes.

"This is my property." Jay clenched and unclenched his fists, which hung down at the level of his hips. "And I'm telling you to get off it. Now."

My dad ignored him. "I had a feeling you were lying to me, Benny. So I wanted to come out here for myself. See the 'patio' you've been building. Hoping to prove myself wrong. But nope. You lied. Just like you do about everything."

"It's not any big deal," I said, acutely aware of my friends watching me and judging me and storing up digs to bug me with later.

"I just knew you were doing bad things out here," my dad said. "Who could guess what you have planned?

Teenaged kids are crazy. Look at that one." He pointed to Jay. "A thug if I ever saw one."

"What the fuck?" Jay broke from the line of our crew and rushed at my father. "What did you call me? On my own property? I could shoot you with the law on my side." Jay didn't slow his momentum when he reached my father, but instead held out his arms and pushed so that my father stumbled back, and as Jay advanced and pushed again, a clamoring panic rose in my chest. At first, I couldn't understand why I was so freaked, but then I realized that my father was tottering straight for our bear trap, that mound of debris that had stopped stinking weeks ago, when some sneaky animal must have gobbled up the rotten hamburger without getting its foot caught.

My dad tripped, his balance already compromised by drink, and fell into the middle of the traps.

"Oh, shit!" I said, rushing towards him, ready to pull off my t-shirt to wrap around the stump of his ankle or wrist.

But he was brushing the leaves off of a trap, trying to see what had cut his shin. The trap hadn't clamped closed, the way it was supposed to. Maybe it had rusted open after all this time, or maybe it had been too old to work in the first place.

"Dad, get out of there," I said and reached out my hand to help him up.

Jay was breathing heavily. A couple of swallows appeared overhead in a dance with each other; they twirled above Jay. "He never comes here again," he said.

My dad looked startled as I pulled him to his feet. Maybe he had sobered some, getting humiliated like that. I worried that he would try to fight Jay or say something else to piss him off, but instead he walked with me through the woods. His shin was bleeding, but not too much. The dirt was alive beneath our feet, alive and decaying, and we both stepped carefully over the uneven surface. He kept quiet, which was worse than him trying to explain it all away, because a new understanding hung heavy between us, this idea that he was weaker than Jay, that Jay came before him in my life.

Once my dad and I got in sight of Jay's house, I turned back. "See you later," I said. He worked his jaw, probably trying to figure out how he could make this my fault.

Finally he came out with, "Stop killing me with the lying."

"You never gave me my allowance," I said. "Not all summer. So I don't see what it is to you."

My dad opened his mouth, but closed it again without speaking. He fumbled with his wallet and handed me a ten dollar bill that smelled of dog food. Alone, I walked slowly along the path, and I wondered if Jay had realized the direction in which he'd pushed my dad, if he'd done it on purpose, trying to finally trap something.

⊏――⊐

Soon after the incident with my dad, Toshi and I headed home. That morning, my bike tire had been flat, so we'd walked. Up in the sky, you could see both the sun and the moon through the tree branches. A few wisps of clouds were catching the sun's light on their pale underbellies, which reminded me of fishing for frogs with my dad, big fat bullfrogs he'd cook up later and call a delicacy. We hadn't fished in years.

"I don't want to go to school tomorrow," Toshi said. "School sucks."

I walked along the edge of the road, careful not to get too close to the ditch.

"All those tests"—Toshi's voice got whinier and whinier —"and the cardboard-tasting cafeteria food, and the rotten bathrooms."

"Just shut up about it."

"You don't have to yell."

The sun was quickly disappearing, and the moon was growing brighter. "At least school will give us something else to do."

"Yeah," Toshi said, "I guess you want to get out of the house."

"I guess you want to shut the fuck up." I took a breath. "I just mean that my dad isn't always like that."

Up in the sky, a little crop duster sputtered and released a cloud of bug juice. The molecules, faintly purple, floated softly to earth.

"It's not really Jay's fault," Toshi said. "Probably, lately, he's been thinking about his brother. It happened in the summer. I mean, that would make me sad all the time, but Jay…"

"What?"

"He's probably been thinking about it because of that thing—you know—when we walked into his house. With his family in the living room."

"No—his brother?"

By then it was mostly dark, but I could sense Toshi staring at me. "He never told you? Sorry; forget I ever said anything. I'm getting one of my headaches; it makes me stupid…"

I wanted to ask Toshi a hundred questions, but I didn't want to admit that I had no idea what he was talking about. "Jay tells me everything," I said. "We're best friends."

We walked the rest of the way home in silence until Toshi handed over my old cast and asked if I wanted it back. "I'm going to stop wearing it," he said. "Tell my dad that it was all healed up so Jay's parents took me to get it cut off. I'll act like it's a miracle my arm is still straight."

"I don't want it," I said and flung the thing into the ditch beside the road.

Chapter 7

On the first day of sophomore year, the three of us met on our usual patch of sidewalk near the parking lot a few minutes before the first bell.

"What's the plan?" I said. We'd spent the whole summer immersed in our town out in the woods, and it felt off-putting to find myself back in regular society.

"Maybe we should move a slab or two closer to the entrance." Jay indicated the sidewalk. "Let the new freshmen have this spot. Move ourselves up in the world."

"I mean about the girls," I said. "About New Veronia."

Tosh nodded.

"That's easy." Jay scooted a few feet towards the school's doors, and we followed. "We all need to convince one girl to come back with us to New Veronia."

"Just like that?" Toshi said.

"Yeah." Jay nodded once. "Right now, I have three maybes. But I have a feeling, like, they might all want to come back with me."

"That's three girls, three of us." Toshi nodded. "Perfect."

"No, no, no; they'd all be mine."

"Do you have condoms?" Toshi said. "Use a condom.

Every year, there are nineteen million new STD cases in our country alone."

Jay said, "You would be lucky to get crabs. But really, come on, we are way ahead of the curve. We're really doing something about getting laid, unlike all these other idiots in our class."

Toshi bumped the case of his horn against his thigh. "But the other guys—they're going to parties and stuff where the girls are."

"Those parties ain't for sex," Jay said. "Those parties are for the girls to crowd into one room and the guys to crowd into another where they can talk about each other among their own."

"That's right," I said to Tosh, though I had wondered myself about what went on in those parties we never got invited to, "we're the only ones taking real action."

Groups of girls stood around us (Stella was in her usual clique underneath the oak tree—sometime soon, I would make my move and apologize to her for my father coming around and bugging her when he was flagged), but not near enough—I hoped—to overhear what we were saying. Besides, they all had their own conversations going, snatches of which I strained to hear, to better understand how I might infiltrate and woo them. One girl screamed something about knee socks, and her friend, who had been in my chemistry class the year before, broke into a fit of laughter. They were inscrutable, all of them. But Jay was right: I had something the other guys at school lacked. I had built New Veronia, and that had to count towards my ability as a boyfriend.

The bell rang and everyone immediately broke from their groups and headed for their first class, a promptness which must have been a product of first-day jitters. I walked to English taught by Ms. Dahl, a new hire. Neither Toshi nor Jay were in the class with me, and I really didn't have any other friends, even though our school had almost three thousand kids attending. Or maybe I didn't have any other friends because our school had so many students. With that many kids, it was hard to single out anyone.

Ms. Dahl proved to be decades younger than I'd suspected, and pretty. Since Stella wasn't in the class—I loved to sit behind her and stare at her shoulders hunched over a textbook—I sat in the front row where I could look at Ms. Dahl's knees, bare beneath her skirt. Her mouth moved, and I nodded, though I wasn't sure what she was saying—my mind was still stuck on New Veronia and women and their legs and all that.

When I went to the bathroom between classes, the place was crowded with seniors. It was only the first day and already they seemed swollen up with power. Every other breath they expelled was a cloud of cigarette smoke, and they hacked yellow loogies into the urinal.

"Piss off," one of them said to me.

"Come on, it's Soppy," his friend said, "and if you don't let him do a little wee-wee, he'll do it in his pants."

I had hoped that maybe everyone would forget about the whole Soppy thing over summer, but I had hoped that every summer for years; people only ever forgot the good stuff about you. I hurried into a stall—I really did need to go— and listened to them all make fun of me ("Maybe he sits down to pee"—"Doesn't want us to see what little he's working with"—"He must be putting on a clean pair of tighty whities"). I felt sort of sick and shaky. Summer had really broken me out of the rhythm of school.

At lunch, I reconvened with Jay and Toshi at one end of a long, plastic table. Jay was talking about soccer.

"We have a real chance to make it to state finals," he said, "with both me and Mark as forwards. I mean, a real chance."

Toshi said, "Do you ever feel mad that the football team gets the band and cheerleaders, and you don't get anything?"

"We don't give a shit about that," Jay said. "It's all about the game."

"I pretend the football team isn't there," Toshi said. "When we play the march, or the fight song, I act like we're on a stage and the audience came to see us."

"That's stupid," Jay said.

"It actually makes me less nervous. At first I used to feel like puking into my horn, and then the thought of that would fill up my mouth with spit, that nauseous sort of spit. I actually have a pretty delicate stomach. And then all of that spit would make it hard to play—"

"I have history last period," I said, "with Stella."

"I can't believe you're still into Stella," Jay said. "I'm going to get her a chastity belt for Christmas."

"Maybe we'll help each other with homework or pair up on a report or something." I finally poked a fork into my cafeteria noodles, which had cooled into an inedible mush.

"Blood is thicker than water," Jay said. "If Stella asks me to call you off, I'd have to do it. No offense."

If Stella and I were betrothed, and we got married, then Jay and I would be brothers. We'd be family. Never again would I have to wonder whether Jay liked me or Toshi more.

"If we can't bring Stella into the fold, if she disgraces the family, she's dead."

The ease with which Jay talked about booting Stella from the family made me wonder about his disappeared brother, the mystery that Toshi wouldn't tell me. "Is that your dad's rule?" I asked Jay as I studied his wrinkled nose, his chapped lips, trying to see if I could sense a long-lost brother somewhere in his face. If Toshi had been telling the truth, then why had Jay kept his brother a secret from me? Obviously, the brother was dead, or had disgraced the family and was now shunned, or maybe he was a hardcore alcoholic lost to the gritty streets of Philadelphia. The brother might have died as a baby, and so he wasn't really important to Jay's life, and Jay had forgotten to mention him to me.

"I got to say"—Jay sucked at his milk—"it's good to have at least one way to kill your sister in your back pocket. It's a survivalist strategy. Just like knowing the ways you could kill a bear—any time, any place—if you had to."

I felt pretty sure I'd never be able to kill a bear *or* my imaginary sister. I dropped my stiff dinner roll back onto the compartmentalized lunch tray.

"Hey Knees, which chick do you have your eyes on?" Jay downed the last of his chocolate milk.

Toshi set down his spork. "I'm thinking… Cindy."

Jay nodded, thoughtful. "Cindy P, or Cindy O?"

"Cindy P."

"Tosh, Tosh, Tosh." Jay belched. "Cindy P is always making this face like her left eyeball is about to fall out."

I laughed in the suppressed way that made soda tingle inside my nose, because it was true: Cindy P made the craziest faces, even when she was doing something ordinary like reciting the pledge of allegiance.

Toshi said, "Maybe, then… Cindy O."

"A good choice," Jay said. "She has a nice rack."

"She really does," Toshi said.

That was when five senior guys came over and told us to get lost; this was their table.

"Come on, man." Jay spoke to the two of them who were on the football team. "I made varsity soccer this year."

I couldn't say anything to back up Jay; if I did, the guys might turn on me and call me Soppy in front of the entire cafeteria.

"Okay?" Jay said. "We'll leave when we're done eating."

Over at the soccer team table, the guys were pretending not to stare at the confrontation. Jay hadn't tried to sit with them, and I wondered why: because he liked me and Toshi more, or because he wanted to sit at a table where he was the most important one, or because the soccer team hadn't offered him a seat?

"You move *now*," the blondest one said. He grabbed the collar of Jay's shirt and pulled.

I was already on my feet, ready to give in, when Jay brought up his fists and made like he was going to plug the guy. The five seniors converged on him before he could swing and pulled him away from the table; there was nothing he could do, being outnumbered like that.

The girls were finally all looking at us as Jay, Toshi, and I walked out of the cafeteria in a tight little group.

Toshi said, "What were you thinking, Jay? You were going to pound all of them and be a hero? You would have gotten pulverized and ended up in the hospital. Sure, you're the smoothest one of us, but that only means you're the smoothest one of the losers."

I stared at Toshi in shock. I'd never heard him be so *mean* before.

"Muzzle up, Knees," Jay said. "If you were any help in a fight, maybe we wouldn't be out here now. And *you*." He pointed at me. "You got your skills from your idiot dad." Jay started stumbling around, tripping over his own feet the way my father had when he'd shown up in New Veronia. "He's running yellow." Jay waved a pretend Nascar flag, then punched the air, letting the momentum of his fist carry him around in a woozy half-circle.

Toshi laughed. "Flagged!" he said.

My face froze somewhere between a grin and a grimace; I wanted to let myself feel bad about the teasing, but if I showed it, they'd only dig in deeper.

Then the bell rang, a jaunty four-note melody that always seemed out of place in the shitty school hallways.

My next class was theater, my favorite. Last year, we did *Midsummer Night's Dream* and the whole jackass mistake was hilarious, the first time I really got into something written hundreds of years ago. I wanted to play Bottom or even be one of the background sprites, but Mr. Blake refused to let me act because I had "dead eyes," and *some*body had to push the button on the CD player backstage. I had hoped that maybe Mr. Blake would die over summer and we'd get a new theater teacher, but there he stood in the middle of the stage. He started reading from the play before he even took attendance.

"'I have lost both my parents,' " he said in a deep voice. And then, raising his voice an octave: "'To lose one parent, Mr. Worthing, may be regarded as a misfortune; to lose both looks like carelessness. Who was your father? He was evidently a man of some wealth. Was he born in what the Radical papers call the purple of commerce, or did he rise from the ranks of the aristocracy?'" He spoke deeply again. "'I am afraid I really don't know. The fact is, Lady Bracknell, I said I had lost my parents. It would be nearer the truth to say that my parents seem to have lost me . . . I don't actually know who I am by birth. I was . . . well, I was found.'" Mr. Blake dipped in a quick bow and a couple of suck-ups belatedly applauded. "And that, students, is the crux of *The Importance of Being Earnest*, by Oscar Wilde, which we will study and perform this semester."

That first class, we did a cold reading of the play, and I got to be the voice of Lane, the Manservant. I had some really hilarious lines, like, "'There were no cucumbers in the market this morning, sir. I went down twice,' " even though I also had to say, "'Yes, sir,' " about a thousand times.

I wished that people talked that way in real life, so that I could pretend I was in a play all the time, where everything was witty and entertaining and inconsequential.

———

That afternoon, I went home and stretched out on the trampoline in the backyard. Years ago, I'd begged my father to get me one, and then he finally had, and it had turned out that I was afraid of the damn thing. After my wrist got broken from the seesaw, I didn't like bouncing so high, not knowing quite how I might land, but the trampoline was a comfortable and convenient spot to stare up at the sky.

It was only four o'clock, so the sun still warmed me, and the younger neighborhood kids were playing some game that involved a lot of yelling, and a few airplane jets spewed their thin, white clouds into the atmosphere. I thought about how I'd known Toshi and Jay for most of my life but really, I didn't know them at all. They were like a tree when the sun starts going down, how the branches and leaves and trunk all turn black even though the sky is blue-orange and lighted behind it, and by the time the tree is no more than a shadow of itself, you're pretty sure that it's a beech, but maybe it's an oak. This was how my oldest friends felt to me.

Earlier that day, I had watched with astonishment as Toshi walked straight up to Cindy O in the hallway and told her that she had a nice rack. He reached out as if he were about to touch it, and when she smacked his hand, he looked at his fingertips like they'd been burnt.

I must have fallen asleep, because when I opened my eyes, it was dark except for the bright yellow square of the kitchen window. My dad was in the kitchen washing something at the sink. I hadn't seen him since he'd stumbled into New Veronia. When I went inside, he said that he was cooking dinner.

"Really?" I said. It seemed like we were going to pretend the incident at New Veronia had not happened, which was fine with me.

"Don't sound so surprised. I cook for you sometimes. Don't I?"

"Sure," I said, because I could tell that he was feeling touchy.

He was making pasta, pouring the box of hard little noodles into a boiling pot. He always said that pasta tasted like wet bread, so he must have been making it because there was nothing else in the house. He set a bottle of ketchup on the counter and, before I could ask, said that we were out of pasta sauce, but ketchup was the base of pasta sauce, anyhow. In a pot, he mixed frozen hamburger with the ketchup, some basil flakes, and dried crumbles of parmesan from the green plastic canister. He added pepper and thyme, and then he drained the noodles and mixed them with the sauce.

The meal was unexpectedly palatable, sweet and salty, or maybe I was especially hungry.

"See?" my dad said when I got up for seconds.

"Yeah, it's pretty good."

"Did I ever tell you that I used to work in a restaurant?"

"No." I really didn't know much at all about my dad when he was growing up, before there was me. And the weird thing was, I didn't feel curious, either—everything I'd ever found out about him was a snore.

"Well, it was really more of a bar. But we sold food. And I was just the prep chef, cutting up potatoes, mostly, but sometimes I threw some plates together. When the chef got to drinking."

"Huh."

"I learned what flavors go together, then. We just don't have anything fresh in the house. If we had a good stocked kitchen, I could really impress you." He stared off into space for a while before asking, "How was the first day of school?"

"Fine." I shrugged, and he didn't nag me for details. He sat there, though, and I felt kind of pinned to my seat. The pasta was gone, and my feet, antsy, tapped at the floor, but I had nowhere to be.

Then he said, "You taking theater again? That was your favorite class last year— wasn't it?"

"I guess." I could feel him staring at me, but I couldn't look up from the red-smeared plate in front of me.

"All right," he said. "I know the first day at school can be rough. Classes okay?"

I filled the air with whatever came into my head. "There are so many hard ones. I don't know if I can... keep up with my grades. And I don't have any classes with my friends. It's not fair: Jay and Toshi have three classes together." I shut up then: I hadn't meant to say Jay's name in front of him.

"That's too bad," my father said.

"I don't know. Can I be excused?" All this attention he was giving me was starting to make me highly uncomfortable. I kept picturing him on the ground, the bear traps all around. If I didn't get away from my dad soon, I felt like I would snap, the way the traps should have. My dad didn't even have to *do* anything to provoke me; for some reason, just him sitting there made my anger flare up. I stood. "Thanks for dinner."

"All right," my dad said, his face the same fleshy mask as always.

Little kids relied on their parents for everything, but they didn't know them at all. They had no idea where their parents went to school or what political party they voted or what was their favorite drink. Then, when the kids got older —when they were my age, for example—they wanted to forget all the things about their parents that they found out. For some reason, it was terrible to know that your dad owned a pair of lucky underwear, that he thought late-night TV was the best, that he once chopped up vegetables for a living, that he drank too much and could get beat up by a fifteen-year-old.

In my room, I put a CD into the player and closed my eyes. The music thrummed in the watery parts of my organs. I took out my ruler and unzipped my pants. My dick was still two little hash marks away from being three inches. When I pushed the ruler as far into my groin as it would go, I gained nine little hash marks, and when I made myself hard, I was five inches, or at a stretch, five and a quarter. This had to be average. Everyone else was probably bragging about his size, or maybe I would get bigger as I got older. Unless I *was* stunted, something to do with my dad not giving me enough testosterone from his side of the equation, and if that was the case, then my life was fucked.

Chapter 8

The girls must have talked among themselves, must have decided that Toshi, Jay, and I were up to something, because on day two of the new school year, the whole female population avoided us like the plague. Or maybe it was only our imaginations, and we were already self-sabotaging our plan to host girls in New Veronia. Because we might have been a little bit scared about what would happen once we got the girls back to the triplex, to our Tony's Mattresses; maybe we worried, at that point, we wouldn't quite know what to do. And if we floundered, we might never be able to show our faces at school again.

"Look at them," Jay said during lunch. We were sitting at the far table, closest to the bathrooms; this was the table that nobody wanted, and so no one would try to kick us off of it. Jay smoothed his hair, but it was too short and just popped right back up. "It's like they have some secret network they can blacklist someone on automatically, just zip-zip, and then you can't get pussy. Just like that."

"Just like that," Toshi repeated, sounding amazed.

"I got to say, bears would do this different. If they're in heat, you *know*. If they want you to chase them around and stuff, you *know*. But us, we need some kind of plan." Jay tapped my forehead. "What we're doing just doesn't work."

"Well," I said. "We have to talk to them, I guess. Be nice. Give them something that they want."

"Something they can *admit* to wanting," Toshi said.

Jay shook his head. "What's that mean?"

"Girls are shallow; they follow these weird rules. Girls aren't supposed to act like they want sex, so they need to say that they'll come to New Veronia for something else, like to check out this thing that we built or drink wine coolers."

"Where can we get wine coolers?" Jay said. "Bennet, you figure that out."

"They like the strawberry flavor," Toshi said. "Even though those things are disgusting."

Jay doodled on a napkin and then handed it to me as if he were a police chief doling out a special assignment.

"I'm on it, sir," I said.

This busted Jay's straight face, and he started laughing, and for a second I felt great, like my police officer persona had been acted to perfection, until Jay said, "That sounded so gay."

When the bell signaled the end of lunch, Toshi followed me down the hall.

"Your class is the other way," I told him.

"I wanted to let you know something," Toshi said.

"How did you learn all that about girls, anyway? Strawberry and shit."

He sighed and hooked his thumbs behind the straps of his backpack. "Clues are in all the TV shows. People want to appear a different way than they actually want to act. It's just human nature."

"Maybe," I said.

"But listen—I wanted you to know: yesterday, in the morning, around ten, your dad drove his truck into my dad's truck. Right in the middle of our street. He was drunk; I mean, really flagged."

"He was at work then," I said; nausea pricked my guts. "And last night he made me dinner. He seemed pretty okay."

"Somebody could have gotten hurt," Toshi said. "It made this big dent. He shouldn't be driving around like that, in that condition."

"Yesterday was a work day."

"And remember in New Veronia? When he showed up? He was drunk then, too. And when we saw him at the liquor store? Alcohol can make you really sick; it's the third most common preventable cause of death in the country."

I started walking towards my class, but Tosh followed. "Are you tattling on him?" I said. "Maybe you should mind your own business." Toshi wasn't trying to humiliate me— he'd told me this away from Jay and everyone else—but I still felt what he was saying like a twist in my gut.

Toshi said, "I only thought you should know." Abruptly

he turned and walked off, towards his next class, before I could think up a response. Watching the back of his head made me want to throw something at it, to explode his glossy hair.

In history, I snagged the desk behind Stella by telling the girl already sitting there that I had problems with my eyesight. Stella was wearing a blue t-shirt with the sleeves rolled up to show off her beautiful arms. I had to get her to talk to me, I just had to, so I asked if she could let me borrow a pencil.

"How come you never come to class prepared?" she said as she handed me the pencil.

"Hey," I said, "I'm really sorry that my dad was bothering you on Sunday. He was… he can be a real bammer sometimes." The frenzy of my heart was making my cheeks twitch, and I dipped my head so Stella wouldn't notice.

"Oh, I know all about dads," she said. "Your dad? That was nothing."

When she turned back around, I put the end of the pencil into my mouth and chewed gently on the eraser. It was like a part of her, a nubbin of her skin against my tongue.

⊏⊐

After school, I hurried straight home and paced the house for a while, thinking about what Toshi had said. My dad might not come home all night, or he might come home while I was asleep and leave before I got up: that had been happening often, lately. But if he was drinking instead of going to work, if he had lost his job, I needed to know *now*.

The last time he'd started to drink during weekdays, we'd been living in Texas, where I was born. He'd sat me down at the eat-in kitchen table, which blocked the sliding glass door, and then he'd explained that we were moving. They'd downsized at his company, and we had to go to Delaware for his new job. I stared out the glass door at the desiccated lawn, where my toy soldiers were lost, permanently stuck somewhere in battle. One week later, my dad pulled me out of the second grade where I had friends, and we left the only house I'd ever lived in, and we gave away my potbellied pig to the neighbors. For years I had a nightmare that they roasted Podge and ate him as soon as our truck pulled away. But the worst part, the part that had truly terrified me, was that my mother would never be able to find us again. She'd left years earlier, but she'd left that house, on that street, in Texas. The walls were still peppered with the decorative crosses that she'd hung up everywhere. If she wanted to, she'd be able to find her way back there. But Delaware? I couldn't be sure that she even knew it existed. Moving away from that house had made me believe that I might never see my mother again.

It wasn't quite four o'clock—my dad got off at five—so I decided to bike to his job.

The employee parking lot of the water treatment plant was still full, and after a quick scan, I didn't see my dad's truck, so I went in to the secretaries at the front desk and asked if they could page him. One of them, an old lady with a crazy perm, squinted at me through her petri dish glasses. "He's not here anymore," she said.

"He's gone for the day?"

"He's just"—she waved her hand through the air —"gone."

"Let go, she means," said a brusque middle-aged secretary.

The linoleum seemed to tilt beneath my feet. It was happening: my life as I knew it was over. My father had been fired; we were going to have to move. I'd lose Jay and Toshi and New Veronia; I'd lose everything.

I biked back to my house in a daze. Maybe we'd have to

move to Alabama now, or Canada, even, or some other awful place. From the end of our driveway, I stared at our little box of a house, tilted slightly to the left, with dirty windows and pieces of the roof flapping in a breeze. But still, it was my home, and I wanted to stay there, because I felt certain that the next place would be worse.

I turned away and biked a few doors down, to Toshi's. I walked in without knocking, like always, and found him perched in front of the computer with the TV on behind him. He was looking up statistics, the only thing he ever used the computer for since his dad had set the parental controls. He said, without taking his eyes from the monitor, "Oh good; you came over. I just got back from hanging out with Jay."

I felt a twinge of jealousy that they had done something without me while I had been watching my world fall apart.

"Did you know there are less than three fatal bear attacks a year? Jay makes it sound like... shit," Toshi said as he finally looked at me, "what's wrong?"

He came and sat beside me on the couch, and we stared at the TV for a while as I struggled to calm myself down. On the screen, men in fatigues were shooting other men in the head. When their skulls broke apart, it sounded like a softball hitting a garage door. A gold tooth fell at the feet of one of the army men.

I took a deep breath. "My dad got fired," I said. "I just found out."

Toshi tilted his head. "That's all? Hey. Come on. I know it sucks, but it's really not a big deal. I thought you were going to say he was in the drunk tank or something and you needed a bunch of money to bail him out."

"You don't understand." Tosh's dad, as a landscaper, got fired from jobs all the time. People would get mad that the yard Toshi's dad created didn't look exactly like the yard they'd pictured in their head, or the job would end up taking three times longer than promised, or the whole tri-state area would be out of blue spruce. "Last time my dad got fired, we had to move. It was horrible. I never saw my friends again."

"Oh, yeah," Toshi said, "how horrible that you met me and Jay."

One of the army men pumped a round into what looked like a woman, but the force of the bullets dislodged a wig, revealing the body as a man's.

"So now I'm going to have to leave the both of you," I said. "And what if, wherever we move, there's no one for me to hang out with? Moving to a new *high school*—that's almost impossible."

After a long time, when the army men had finished the job and were celebrating with whiskey, Toshi said, "Maybe you have everything wrong, and you'll get to stay in this crappy town. It's full of asbestos here anyway. It will be okay. Everything will work out; you'll see."

I said, "You don't understand. You don't have any idea."

Toshi made his face like a carp's, those unblinking, sad eyes, that mouth open in a way that made you think there was only slick nothingness all the way down.

I waited up for my father; I wasn't going to let him sneak into his bedroom without telling me what was going on. When he came in, the time was almost one in the morning. He wasn't expecting to see me: when he did, he stumbled a little, and then he threw back his shoulders and walked slowly and deliberately.

"Bennet," he said, "you're up late. Isn't this a school night?"

"Dad, where have you been?"

He shrugged. "Out with friends."

I knew that this was a lie: my father had no friends. Maybe there were a few guys from work he'd drink with on occasion, but now he didn't have coworkers. "Where have you been, really?"

"At the roadhouse." He shrugged again.

"I went by the plant today."

He stood awkwardly in the middle of the living room, and I swear I saw the throb of his pulse quicken in the groove alongside his neck. Finally he said, "Why would you do that?"

"I found out that you got fired."

"That's not true," he said. "That's not true at all."

Infuriated, I clenched and unclenched my fists, then chewed rhythmically on the inside of my own cheek. "Is this why you were so weird to me about that fake patio, at Jay's house? You kept complaining that I lied—is that because you've been lying to me about everything?"

"No, that's different—I'm not lying." My dad strode into the kitchen and got a beer. "You're the kid; you can't lie to me." He snapped off the cap and gulped from the bottle.

"I went there," I said. "To the plant. They told me."

"Who told you? Carol? That woman is batty."

The fury stormed around inside me; I could feel it shoving my insides.

"I don't know what you think you figured out," my dad said. "But whatever it is, you're wrong." He leaned against the fridge as if this were any old casual conversation.

My head started a powerful ache. "Then why are you drinking so late at night? If you have to go to work tomorrow?"

"I'm not going to let a punk kid like you tell me what to do. You're *wrong*, Bennet. I'm still working. Placed on a special assignment, lately. Schedule shifted around a little."

Maybe I was hearing things; maybe those women in the front office had my dad confused with someone else, or they didn't know about the special assignment. That one lady *had* seemed pretty senile. Maybe all the stress of trying to get girls and starting school again was messing with my reality. "Are you sure?" I said. "You'd tell me otherwise?"

"I swear to god."

I didn't understand how my father could always sound so right; maybe it was a skill I would learn with age, too.

He said, "But I do have something I've been meaning to tell you."

A hot wave of anticipation compressed my stomach. "What is it?"

"I want you to be excited about this, I really do. I want you to be… happy about something for once."

"I'm happy," I said. "What is it?"

"I want you to be happy because of something I did." He pinched the skin above his nose, and fine wrinkles appeared across his forehead.

"What did you do?" A heaviness descended on my body, like every part of me had fallen into an exhausted sleep except for my overactive worry.

"Dammit." He swayed a little on his feet. "I didn't even do it. Actually, it wasn't even me. It was your mother. Your mother called."

The lamp in the corner brightened as if in a surge of electricity, and I squinted my eyes against it. "She what?"

"Called. On the phone."

His toneless voice sent a fast thrill through me. "She hasn't called in…"

"I know," my father said.

We paused there in the now-dim-again light and waded through our own thoughts. My mother's voice was husky, or it used to be—maybe she'd quit smoking cigarettes by now.

My father sat down next to me on the couch, but not so close that we were in any danger of touching. All of a sudden, I felt disgusted that he had a body with hair and snot and thousands of dead skin cells, a body that had rubbed against my mother. I didn't see how kids with two parents living in the same house, sleeping together in the same bedroom, could stand the constant reminder of geriatric sex. I scooted to the furthest cushion, away from him.

"She wants you in October. You can go to school in Florida, where she's living; she lives right next to a school, a good school."

I closed my eyes, which had started to feel like two raisins pressed into my skull. It was funny how they could seem dried out when all that I wanted to do was cry.

"And while you're gone," he said, "I might take a trip. I've been thinking about going away for a little while."

"A trip."

"Yeah, a road trip, in October, when you go to stay with your mother. Raising a kid by myself, I haven't been able to take any trips. But before all that happens, think about this: we'll have a month and a half together, you and me; we can do whatever you'd like. It will be fun, probably, the two of us."

My body was hot; my body was cold; the temperatures swirled together and made me feel kind of crazy. "When is the last time we did something fun? Why don't you just go now? Pack up your truck and leave. I'm old enough. I'll be fine."

"Benny, don't act like that. Come on."

"Don't call me a baby name just because you don't want me to be mad at you." The angry heat moved through me in waves.

"Listen, we can talk about this in the morning. Okay?" He stood up like an old man, pressing his hands against his knees to help with leverage. "We're both tired. We need some rest. Then we can talk." He disappeared into the back of the house.

Even if I slept for a hundred years, I wouldn't be able to really talk to my dad: just like when older kids had tortured me on the playground, or when I'd convinced myself a lump on my head was cancer, or when I'd become weirdly depressed after I ran over this cute little mouse thing on my bike and killed it, I would keep to myself. The couch pillow dented beneath my fist over and over again, the sound of the thing being crushed no more than a sad little whoosh.

That night, I couldn't sleep; I thought about the time I'd decided to join a church to feel closer to my mother. When we'd lived in Texas, she would go to this Catholic church every Sunday, a big, dark-stone place. She'd take me with her in a stroller and sit me on her lap during the ceremony so that she could clamp a hand over my mouth if I cried. Her fingers always tasted of vanilla from the lotion she carried in her purse. In Delaware, when I was eleven, I went through this phase of missing her that I decided to address with a trip to church. I found a Catholic church, white clapboard, but with a couple of stained glass windows that reminded me of the place back in Texas. At the Sunday service, the priest's sermon about Mary, mother of Jesus, sounded like a lecture. When everyone lined up to take communion, I followed, but I could feel the old ladies' eyes burning into me. One of them stepped on the back of my shoe and this made me want to crumple up and explode at the same time. They didn't want to welcome me at all. Since then, I had pretty much stopped missing my mother, stopped obsessing over her, until now, with my dad throwing her back into my life.

Chapter 9

The following morning, when I left for school, my dad was still asleep in his room. I waffled between the possibility that he was okay, just on a special assignment; or that he'd gotten fired, and the "special assignment" excuse let him pretend that he didn't have to go to work until later.

At school, Toshi and I met up in our usual spot and stood around, waiting for Jay. "I have to go down to Florida," I told him, "in October."

"For what?" Toshi said. "Vacation? Last year, there were six reported cases of malaria in Florida. I wouldn't go."

"I've never gone anywhere for vacation."

"Oh no," Toshi said and bit his bottom lip, "did your dad really get fired? And you have to move right away, just like you thought?"

"It's not that. I'm staying with my mom for a little bit."

He clutched at the case of his French horn as if it were something precious. "Are you *serious*? That's going to be weird. I mean, you haven't seen her in…"

"Tosh, stop sounding like a little prick just because my mom actually wants to see me."

He curled up into himself then, and I took pleasure in

the way his face crumpled like a used-up paper bag. Everyone at school would see that he was the weak one, the wannabe mama's boy, not me.

I left him there, looking pathetic, and walked towards Stella and Jay, who had just arrived. Compared with Toshi, I was a real man; Stella should be able to see that. Since I was leaving mid-semester, it meant I needed to convince her to come with me to New Veronia, and fast.

But just as I entered Stella's bubble of candy perfume, I veered away, towards Jay. I had no idea what to say; Stella and I never conversed in front of other people. I needed Jay. A pep talk. He would help me figure out what to do.

We cut first period: Jay showed me how to wait in the bathroom until a few minutes after the bell rang and then just walk out the double doors. I'd never really cut class before—I'd always felt afraid of what I might miss—but none of it mattered now. I was leaving this place.

We sat in a far corner of the football field and Jay concentrated on the problem of pussy. "You can't move away, man, not when we're so close to getting some. *So close.* I mean, how long will this whole situation last? When are you coming back? Are you definitely coming back?" As he spoke, he picked at a scab on his elbow.

"Of course I'm coming back," I said, before realizing that I really didn't know. Florida was so far away. My dad might disappear on the road, or get into a car crash, or decide he didn't want me anymore. I was that kind of kid, I guess.

I plucked some grass and threw it down. "Remember what you said before about kicking Toshi out of our group?"

"Yeah."

I waited, but Jay, working on his scab, kept silent.

I shrugged. "Everything has to happen fast, now. Maybe we *should* ditch Tosh. Do you think he's holding us back on getting girls?" It seemed like Jay and Toshi had been hanging out together without me more often, lately, and that worried me: what if Jay decided *I* was the one to kick out of the group? What if he forgot me after I left?

"Sometimes it's better to keep someone close," he said. "You get what I mean? Keep an eye on them that way."

My stomach fell: Toshi wasn't going anywhere. Maybe Jay did like Toshi better than me. Toshi would be around to make sad faces and worry over my dad's drinking and steal away Jay's attention until I left, and then it would be just the two of them. They could share secrets about Jay's mystery brother, the one he'd never told me about. None of it was fair. I said, "Yeah, well. Now that I'm moving in October, the main thing is, we have a deadline. For New Veronia."

"Absofuckinglutely we do," Jay said. He flicked his scab to the ground. "And the sooner, the better, for me. I mean, I can't wait. I really can't."

"Yeah," I said, "me, too." The way all the girls stood in a tight, impenetrable circle on the blacktop made me despair every morning, but if Jay really put his mind to it, I knew that we could get some of them out to New Veronia. "Hey— do you think that you could talk to Stella for me? Maybe, just —convince her to come out? For me?"

"I don't get why you want that cum dumpster so bad," Jay said. "And she's my sister and I love her and all that shit, I guess, but she's slept with like a hundred guys, some black guys too." He smeared the blood that had welled up where the scab used to be across his elbow. "And I might have to punch you or something. If you get dirty with my sister."

"That doesn't make any sense. I mean, you plug those other hundred guys?"

"It's cause I know you would tell me about it," he said. "And then I'd have to punch you."

No question this would be worth it, for Stella. She was perfect, the perfect woman, and the danger of my loving her only added to her allure.

After school, we all convened in New Veronia. Toshi had brought some vodka he'd found in the back of a cabinet at his house; he'd never gotten us anything to drink before.

"Thanks, man, this is perfect," Jay said. We were all in his part of the triplex, which had ended up just a little bit bigger than the others. I pushed aside some of Jay's clothes and sat on the mattress; Jay balanced atop a rickety old stool he'd brought over from his garage.

"Are we supposed to save this stuff for the girls?" I asked, passing Jay the bottle.

He threw down the magazine he'd been flipping through. It landed atop a bunch of other junk—blanket, soccer ball, portable radio—that he'd scavenged from his house. "They wouldn't drink it," he said. "Keep working on the wine coolers."

When Jay passed the bottle to me, I wrapped my lips around it, preparing mentally for the burn in my throat and the jump of nausea in my stomach.

"You know that girl, Janet, with the super-shiny lips?" Jay said. "She would come out here with me next weekend, but I have to go to this thing with my parents. So she'll come the next week. You two need to get girls, too, so she doesn't feel alone or whatever."

"Where are you going with your parents?" I asked, avoiding the real question about how Toshi and I were supposed to get girls.

"Some conference thing. Something political. They go every year, and I'm old enough now to be a part of the conference, too. To have a political conscience."

"Oh," I said. My dad and I had never gone anywhere together, not really. We'd taken a couple of day trips to fish frogs and once we'd seen the phonograph museum, but we hadn't done anything that lasted for a whole weekend, and though my dad had said we could hang out before he packed me off to my mother, he was all talk. "Where is it?"

"Kentucky," Jay said. "Takes over a day to drive. I'll get to miss some school."

"Killer," Toshi said.

"Is Stella going?"

"Whole family."

"When you go on a trip like that, do you guys, like, stay in the same room? Same hotel room? You and Stella?"

"You're one sick fuck, Bennet." Jay laughed. "This trip is a big deal. All kinds of important guys will be there, and I'm going to meet them. They all know my parents. I mean, my parents are more big into this kind of thing than you would think. And it's time to start growing up."

Dave the squirrel scampered across the outside wall; the scritch of his little claws had become a familiar noise, and sometimes we stuck peanuts in the cracks for him.

"Maybe we could start a housebuilding company," Jay said. I could smell the sweet, harsh vodka on his breath. "When we graduate."

With a pang, I thought that maybe I would have to graduate in Florida, far away from everything I knew.

"Or we could drop out and do it now. After soccer season is over."

"A long time ago," Toshi said, "I promised my mom I would graduate. Forty-two percent of homeless teenagers are high school dropouts."

"Oh wait, I didn't tell you?" Jay grabbed the bottle back from me. "I've actually been keeping your mom in my basement so that I can slip it to her on the sly. You should go down there and ask *her* for some more life advice."

This was Jay's brand of sarcasm, and we laughed along with him.

"Or maybe if we're housebuilders," Toshi said thoughtfully, "that would keep us from being homeless. We could build a super-sturdy New Veronia."

"That's dumb." Jay came and sat on the bed so that we all bounced. "In a few years, we won't need a New Veronia. We'll have wives and houses, and we can just take them into the bedroom and fuck them there."

"I wouldn't be so sure," Toshi said. "You never know what might happen, years from now. We could be in another depression. People living in tents."

When the bottle of vodka was nearly empty, we all flopped back on the bed and stared up at the overlapping wood slats of the sloped ceiling. As I watched the planks, they spun a few degrees, then snapped back into place. My head felt pleasantly light, and I breathed through my nose because it made the air cooler.

"Knees"—Jay held out the vodka—"you finish the bottle."

It occurred to me that Toshi hadn't had any, or maybe he'd had just a sip. Anyway, he couldn't be feeling as unsteady on his feet as I did.

"No, thanks," Toshi said. "I'm starting to get a headache."

Jay spun the vodka bottle around on the bed; it pointed at Tosh. "Look at that," he said. "Now you have to do whatever I say."

"I think that maybe Bennet wants it."

I shrugged. "I'm okay."

Toshi cut his eyes over to me. "The children of alcoholics are four times more likely to be alcoholics themselves."

"What the fuck, Tosh?" I said. Probably all the dads in our neighborhood drank just like mine. The second shelf of every fridge I'd ever opened was full of Sam Adams. In Delaware, dads loved beer and they loved the Founding Fathers, too.

"Drink it, Knees," Jay said.

I hurried upright so that I wouldn't miss the show. The quick movement made my head twirl. I felt pissed at Toshi for always harping on my father, and I wanted him to suffer a little bit so that he'd feel the way I felt.

Toshi held the bottle like it was a used hanky, but Jay didn't have to say anything else to make him drink: Jay just narrowed his brown eyes until the staring bore into Toshi's brain.

Toshi dumped the bottle's contents into his throat, and then he choked and sputtered and let at least half of it dribble back out over his chin.

"You," Jay said, "are the biggest pussy I have ever known. In fact, I think you're reaching vagina level. I mean, do you got boobs?"

"No," Toshi said angrily, which was a mistake: he should have stayed quiet.

"Well, obviously you didn't do my dare. You spit up half the booze like a baby." Jay rolled his shoulders so that the bones cracked. "So now you got to do another one."

"I didn't know we were playing truth or dare," Toshi said, again when he should have just shut up.

"I dare you to go outside, run around the cabin, and come back in." Jay rummaged around beside his mattress and then held up a jar of peanut butter. "With this smeared on you. Bear bait."

"Whatever," Toshi said, which would have been on the right track, except for his eyes turned red and watery. Jay hated those sorts of signs of weakness.

"Now," Jay said, "take off all your clothes."

Toshi stripped down to his underwear and reached for the peanut butter, but Jay said no. "*All* your clothes."

Toshi protested, he squirmed, but in the end, he did as Jay said.

It surprised me that Toshi's penis was a dark purplish color, and it was uncut, which surprised me even more.

Halfway down, it curled a little to the right, and I thought about a snail backing into its shell. But as he ducked outside, I had this flash of déjà vu, like I'd seen his dick before a long, long time ago. Playing around when we were little kids, had we turned our dicks into toys? Had we pretended to fire them at each other, like guns? It bothered me that my elephant recall was glitching out now, that I couldn't figure out if this was a false memory, or something that had really happened. Maybe the vodka was interfering with my recollection.

While Toshi was outside humiliating himself in the dark night air, Jay and I catcalled for bears. I laughed until my cheeks were two painful knots on either side of my face. And after Toshi's ordeal was over, Jay gave him a noogie, rubbing his hair affectionately, until they forgave each other and we were ready to move on.

Toshi, just perceptibly dazed, zipped his fly and smoothed his shirt. "What are we doing tonight?"

―――

It turned out that Jay's soccer guys were having a party because the goalie's parents were out of town, and so we walked the three miles there and let ourselves in the front door. My stomach bubbled with nervous energy: we'd never really gone to a party like this before, and though we talked shit about them, that was secretly because we'd never been invited.

The house was two stories with low ceilings and a series of small rooms: den, living, dining, kitchen, laundry.... In one room there were girls from the volleyball team, another held football guys, another had kids dancing. We went to the kitchen and found a couple of beers; Toshi didn't want one.

"Ladies!" Jay said as he walked back into the den. He drew out the word for a long time, as if it were a lyric.

Some of the girls glanced over at us, but none of them smiled. The air smelled strongly of cotton candy from their perfume, and I wanted to run a hand across the backs of their heads to test the stiffness of their hair. I was still floating inside the fumes of the vodka we'd drank back at New Veronia.

"What's going on in here?" Jay walked over to the couch and sat on its arm; then he leaned into a blond girl named Myra, sort of falling on her lap, pretending to be drunker than he was. "Hey," he said, "whoops!" In trying to right himself, he only rubbed up against her more.

Feeling stupid, I stood beside Toshi in the doorway.

"About your mom," Toshi said. "I can't believe you're leaving. Is she remarried? Aren't you worried that you don't know her anymore? Like you'll be living with a stranger?"

"Ashley," I said as a girl I knew slightly from freshman English class walked down the hallway. No way was I going to stand around at a party and talk to Toshi about my feelings for my mommy. "Hey—what's new?" I followed her as she made her way toward the kitchen. "It's Bennet. Remember? We studied *The Great Gatsby* for basically the whole semester? 'In his blue gardens men and girls came and went like moths among the whisperings and the champagne and the stars.' " When I'd first read it, that line had struck me with its loneliness, and I'd gone over it and over it as if it were my part in a play. But Ashley didn't seem impressed by the quote, even though girls were supposed to be into that stuff. "I wish we could go to a party more like that, you know, with champagne."

"Right," she said. She stopped just short of the kitchen and people pushed around us. "I remember you: you look exactly the same."

My toes curled inside their sneakers, and the alcohol-confidence ticking through my veins immediately evaporated. Ashley did not look exactly the same: her tits had gotten bigger and she'd dyed the bottom half of her hair an unnatural red. I felt like I was the only teenager not changing, not growing up, like some freak in the type of movie divorcees watched on weekday afternoons. I sort of wanted to stomp on Ashley's foot, but I wanted her to like me, too, so I bit my lip instead.

I was just starting to tell Ashley about New Veronia when I heard Jay yelling.

Back in the den, I found Jay standing in a corner, both hands held up and palms out, with three of his soccer teammates standing in front of him.

"Who told you that you were invited, man?" asked the one with his arm around Myra. His name was Mark; he was a forward. I sort of remembered overhearing something about Mark and Myra getting together, that their love was like candy, M&Ms. "Did anyone invite you?"

"It's a *soccer* party." Jay was swelling up in his corner; his muscles were pumping with anger. "I'm *on* the team."

"We don't consider you part of the team," the goalie said. "After what you did to my little bro. What's wrong with you, man?"

"But for reals," Mark said, "get out."

The three of them started towards Jay, but he moved faster; he broke through their line and was across the threshold.

"And you too, Soppy." Mark pointed at me. "And your little friend. *Out.*"

Toshi and I glanced at each other; we had been moving towards the door already. Mark only wanted to yell at us to make our banishment more humiliating. The doorknob stuck a little, which gave everyone three more seconds to laugh at us.

We found Jay panting at the end of the neighbor's driveway. His pacing around like a caged tiger reminded me of this strange illustration from the bible: "for those who exalt themselves will be humbled, and those who humble themselves will be exalted." It took me a long time of looking at the illustration to decide that it was God who'd switched out the men and the tigers to punish the men for thinking that they were superior.

"Those bammers," Jay said. "Those fucking *bammers*."

He'd never talked bad about any of the soccer guys before, it was always *they told me this* and *they did that* and *their girlfriends are so hot.*

"They think they can kick me out when they're nothing special."

My body felt numb. Over summer, I'd sort of forgotten that, at school, Jay wasn't killer at all, because he was definitely the best, the leader, of our crew. But Toshi had been right: we were a group of losers, and being a king of losers still made you a loser. This realization sat, uncomfortably heavy, in the pit of my stomach. Maybe it was dumb, how much I admired Jay, how I sometimes wished that I could be him.

Jay snorted in anger. "Who do they think they are?"

Not even Jay's team liked him, and his making varsity soccer hadn't changed that fact at all. "Yeah," I said, "those bammers."

"We're going to get them," Jay said. "Get them back."

"But what did you do to that guy's brother?" Toshi asked.

"Nothing much. Just a little hazing. The kid is a freshman, for fuck's sake."

"You hazed him?" Toshi said slowly.

"We were in the shower. All I did was pee on him a little bit. He could clean it right off! We were showering!"

I wrinkled my nose and said, "A freshman is on varsity soccer?"

"He's not even that good. Only made it because he's got connections, with his brother on the team. It's not fair he has someone looking out for him like that. They stick together, you know, in this creepy sort of way."

As a freshman, Jay hadn't been able to make varsity soccer; maybe this kid's success rankled him.

"That Mark is such a taint. *Get out, get out,*" Jay mocked. "*He's* going to get it. Let's fill some soda bottles with our piss and explode it in the middle of their party."

And just like that, Jay was back with his plans and his momentum and his energy. Jay's stupid teammates hadn't taken the time to get to know the Jay I knew, the one who always thought up the next fun thing. He wasn't a loser, not really; it was just the crappiness of high school that made him seem like one. Which meant, as Jay's right hand man, I wasn't a total social failure, either. Even if we were outside the party, the three of us were outside it together.

"Probably the stuff will explode all over us instead," Toshi said, sounding kind of butt-hurt.

"You know how to make a bomb?" I asked.

⸻

Dry ice was the key ingredient. By the time we came back with some an hour and a half later, the party was in full swing. Jay had made us all drink a bottle of Mountain Dew because he claimed that it made the foulest-smelling piss, and as we walked the last block, my bladder hung low and heavy. Our plan would be the ultimate revenge for those assholes calling me Soppy.

We heard the noise from two houses away: steady drum-beat from a stereo, kids yelling, a bottle breaking against cement.

"We'll approach from behind," Jay whispered, though nobody at the party would have heard us even if he'd yelled; they were busy having too much fun. He led us through a soybean field to the backyard of the house, which was demarcated by the end of the crop. We crouched in the dark-ness at the edge of the stalks; the wind kept pressing the green leaves against my back where my shirt rode up and left my skin uncovered.

Kids were all over the backyard, some leaning against the vinyl siding and smoking cigarettes, some making out on the strip of lawn between the house and shed, some rolling around on the ground acting super wasted. Plastic cups peppered the grass like strange, red flowers.

"Got to be careful with this shit," Jay said as he opened the package of dry ice. The inch-long cylinders were shrink-ing, sending their mass into the air as smoke. "Could burn your finger off." He plucked a soybean leaf and used it as a barrier between his skin and the cylindrical ice cubes, then dropped as many pieces as would fit into the empty Mountain Dew containers. "Now we piss into it, screw on the lid, and throw it right into the middle of them." He indicated the revelers.

"Then what?" Toshi said.

"Ka-boom! They get piss-bombed."

Peeing into the soda bottle turned out to be more difficult than I would have thought, mainly because I had to go so bad that it rushed from me in a hard and fast stream rather than an easily managed dribble. The stink was like asparagus mixed with liver.

"Fuck." Jay was having the same problem, and he'd sprayed on his shoes. Toshi, on the other hand, wasn't peeing at all.

"Maybe you have to pull back the foreskin," I told him.

"He's just nervous," Jay said. "Don't want to pee in front of people."

In a flash, all the times Tosh and I had been in a bathroom together zipped through my memory: Jay was right; Toshi was pee-shy. Now that I thought about it, Toshi had never taken a piss in front of me. My brain throbbed to realize something that I basically must have known for years.

"That's okay," Jay said, screwing a cap on his bottle. "I got enough for both of them."

Once our bottles were full, their contained ecosystems swirling with vaporous white clouds, we each took one and flung them as far as we could towards the house. Jay aimed his for where Mark and Myra were drinking on the steps. It landed close, and when it plopped down, Mark and another soccer guy moved in for a look.

"Oh fuck!" Jay said in an ecstatic whisper. "They're going to get piss in the face!"

Then one of them reached down and picked up the bomb as if it were a bottle of liquor fallen from heaven.

"Shit! Shit! Shit!" Jay said.

My heart was clawing its way up my throat when Mark

unscrewed the lid, releasing all pressure on our piss bomb. I deflated, and not even watching his nose wrinkle up in disgust after he sniffed the stuff made me feel better.

But then, the other two bombs exploded, one right after the other. The liquid shot up ten feet into the air and then fell back down as acid rain. Girls screamed, people clawed at their pissed-on skin, Mark glared like a bear about to rampage.

And then the three of us were bolting through the soybean field, whooping because, even though it would have been smarter to stay quiet, we couldn't help ourselves.

The whole walk back home, we told each other the story over and over again. The Mountain Dew containers kept growing bigger, our piss concoction getting nastier, the threat of Mark inching closer. A sort of frenzy took over my body as I flailed my arms, retelling, but I wasn't alone: Jay and Toshi were flagged on the memory, too.

Jay wrapped his arm around Toshi's neck and noogied his head. "This guy," he said, "this guy couldn't even pee! How's your bladder doing, huh, Knees? About to explode inside you? Or has it been stretched out enough by now?"

Toshi wriggled out from under Jay's knuckles. "You won't laugh once I get *sepsis*."

"When they blew up," Jay said, "Mark had no idea what to do. He would never be able to survive in a war. I bet his dad never even taught him to *shoot*."

After Jay peeled off from our group to head back to his house, Tosh and I sobered up. The night air crept through my clothes and chilled my skin, and I tried to remember if Mark had looked directly at us, if he'd seen our outlines against the soybeans. "If we get caught," I said, "we are so dead."

"You should pull some kind of big prank right before you leave for Florida." Toshi's voice got higher, the way it did when he thought he had a good idea. "Then you'll hop on the plane, and no one will ever know it was you. Or if they do find out, it won't matter: you'll be long gone."

I hadn't ever flown on a plane before, but I'd always wanted to try that up-high feeling which would probably paint a gloss over all the small, annoying junk down on earth. "I wonder if my mom already bought me the ticket." I'd just assumed that I'd have to take the bus down, or maybe my dad would drive me as part of his road trip.

Toshi said, "Sometimes I worry that, if my mom ever picked me up at the airport, I'd have no idea which person she was. I mean, I really might not recognize her. Only sixteen percent of children from divorced households live with their fathers. Sixteen. You're the only other one I've ever met."

"Whatever," I said. Toshi had a one-track mind, but at least he'd waited until Jay was gone to get all mushy about our moms. He still smelled like peanuts from his bear-bait dare, and this made him seem smaller and sadder than usual.

"You should ask her about your family medical history. When you get older, the doctors are going to want that."

"What's with you?" I said. "It's no big deal. I'm going away for a little while. I'll come back; everything will be normal." Maybe I was starting to feel scared, then, because pretty soon I would have to leave everything familiar, and I stop feeling scared by getting angry. I'd been thinking about my mom for too long, so long that she'd become an idea, and the thought of actually living with this idea disturbed me. "You jealous that my mom didn't leave the country to get away from me? I don't need a passport to go see her? I don't even *want* to see her. This is all about her; *she* wants to see *me*."

Toshi nodded; you could walk all over him and he'd

never get in your face about it. "Jay is right about you," I said.

Toshi stopped in the middle of the empty road. "The only reason Jay is harder on me than on you is because he cares about me more overall."

I stood in front of Toshi and stared up into his face, trying to dagger him with my eyes. "What a nice, delusional fantasy world you live in. Get a clue, Toshi. Jay doesn't really care about you. In fact, this summer, he was talking about kicking you out of our group! He doesn't want you around anymore, but he puts up with you because you would fall apart if we ditched you."

"He didn't," Toshi said and rubbed at his temples. "It's always been the three of us."

"You embarrass us. You're weird; you're not really one of us. We're sick of you." I left him then, marching on ahead, and for about a hundred steps, I felt good for asserting my position as Jay's only real friend, and then for the next hundred steps, I felt a little queasy, and then an image of Toshi's thin xylophone of a chest smeared with peanut butter flashed through my mind, and I felt downright terrible about what I'd said, but there was no taking it back, now, not without making me look like just as much of a wimp as Tosh.

Chapter 10

The Monday following the party, everyone at school was talking about the piss bombs; the rumor was that the rival high school soccer team had done it. People said there had been ten bombs, or twenty, and some of them had been filled with hot sauce or shit or little pieces of metal. I felt like a secret celebrity, which was nice, though it would have been killer to be a non-secret celebrity, to have everyone at school know my real name for once.

But in fifth period, when my name, along with Toshi's and Jay's, was called over the loudspeaker, fear filled my chest.

The principal gathered us into her office. "We take acts of terrorism very seriously at this school," she said.

Jay shook his head. "Terrorism?"

"Shut your mouth. What the three of you did on Saturday night was unacceptable. It was a biohazard, too."

"And what is it that you think we did?" Jay's voice was hard, which didn't help his case any in the principal's eyes.

"You're off the team," she said. "We don't need a hooligan like you representing our school in sports."

"No." Jay wriggled like a trapped animal. "That's not fair, seriously. I didn't *do* anything."

The principal had it all planned out: at the right moment in her little speech, the police barged in and dropped their meaty hands onto our shoulders. One of them was the D.A.R.E. officer, and he looked way happier than he did when he was up on the assembly stage telling all us kids why drugs were bad. The officers hauled us out to their squad car, then shoved the three of us into its backseat. Beside me, Toshi shivered and gnawed his bottom lip. It felt like I'd been dropped inside a movie and the whole façade would fall away at any moment, but when I pressed against the door of the police car, it stayed solid and unmoving.

"What the hell is happening?" I said. The police were standing on the sidewalk, gossiping with the principal. "How are they allowed to do this?"

"I told Mark it was us," Jay said. His distress blew through the air like a hot wind.

"You did *what?*"

"That pussy bammer must have told on us. What kind of man snitches like that?"

"Everyone thought it was Dover High!" I said. "Why would you ruin that?"

"It was a killer idea," Jay said, "and it was mine. If the wrong people get credit, that takes away half the fun. When Mark found out that it was *my* piss in his eyes—you should have seen him freak."

Toshi whimpered.

"We are in so much trouble," I said as the policemen let themselves into the car.

"They can't really kick me off the team." Jay shook his head. "They can't; there's no way. It wouldn't be fair. Besides, they *need* me."

At the station, a lady police officer took each of our fingers and rolled them across a pad of ink, then across a sheet of paper. She was kind of pretty, and normally, having her touch my hand like that would have given me a boner, but I was too scared.

They took our pictures with a slew of numbers held beneath our chins, and then we were handcuffed to a bench in the hall.

After maybe an hour, an officer came to talk with us.

"How does it feel to be treated like real criminals, boys?" he said.

"We didn't do it!" Toshi blurted out. "One in twenty-five on death row are innocent. It's easy to get it wrong."

The officer rolled his eyes. "I know everything. And I know that I have enough on you to keep you here in jail."

"It was just a prank," I said. "It wasn't terrorism or whatever. Nobody got hurt, right?"

"You need to understand there are repercussions to your actions," the officer said. "You're lucky we caught you so that you can figure out early on how criminals get punished. I'm going to leave you to think about what you did. Think about how to be men." He walked away and poured himself a cup of coffee, and we didn't see him again for three hours. At first, we speculated about whether or not they could trace piss the way they could blood, and Toshi, on the verge of tears, kept sucking snot back up into his nose. Then we all fell quiet and restless and I tried to only think about the pinch of my wrist inside the handcuff.

When the officer finally came back, he said that we each could have a phone call. "Get someone to come pick you up. I want you out of my sight."

He uncuffed Jay first and led him over to a phone a couple of yards away while I said, "Wait—we can go? You're letting us go?"

The police officer watched Jay dial. "Dad," Jay said, and, "yes. Yes. Yes. Okay."

When Jay was beside me, again manacled to the bench, he said, "My dad won't come. He's mad I'm off the team. He's real mad."

But Toshi's dad said he'd come for all three of us, which was good, since my dad didn't answer.

Standing on the sidewalk in front of the police station, Tosh said, "I think they were just trying to scare us. I don't think they had any intention of keeping us in jail, but they wanted to make it seem really serious with the mugshots and the fingerprinting."

"My dad never came to one of our games," Jay said, "but still I think he hates me. Now I don't play. That *bitch* principal."

"There's my dad," Toshi said. "Pulling up in the parking lot. I bet he's going to ground me, no book or horn or anything. Probably my skull will collapse from boredom."

Jay glanced at the rows of cars, then stared in the opposite direction. "I'm walking."

"What?"

"I can't be cooped up in no car right now."

I sort of felt like following him, but I knew it was a long walk, and the ordeal had left me bone-tired.

"I still don't believe you," Toshi said to me as we watched Jay getting smaller. "That Jay doesn't want me around anymore."

"Whatever," I said.

Chapter 11

Jay was sprung from class early on Thursday to go with his family to that conference in Kentucky. During lunch, while I stared at Jay's empty seat, I thought about the time in third grade when his parents had come for him, the possessive way they steered him off. Jay seemed to belong to his family more than I did to mine, but maybe that was because my family was just my dad—not really enough people to make an actual one.

After school, Toshi and I met up, but without Jay there, we weren't sure what to do with ourselves. We only talked about him.

"I wonder if they'll drive straight through," Toshi said.

"All the way to Kentucky?"

"That's how people get aneurysms. They don't move their legs, and their blood clots…"

In front of Jay, Toshi and I had pretended to be friends, but now that he was absent, I wasn't sure if I should keep pretending that things were fine—only, I wasn't even sure that things *weren't* fine. Toshi was still a part of our crew, and now that Jay was gone, I wouldn't have had anyone to stand beside if not for Tosh. Maybe Toshi talking shit about my dad being a drunk, and me telling Tosh that he was weird, that Jay wanted him out of our group, was ultimately inconsequential, just like the fight we'd gotten into in the sixth grade over my Gameboy that I said Toshi had broken and Toshi said was broken already. I had hated him fiercely for about three days, and then all my anger had disappeared, and we were normal again.

I decided to aim for normal. "Who do you think he knows at this conference? Older people? Or does he have a special group of friends like you when you go to camp?" I didn't have anyone outside of Toshi and Jay.

"They're probably older people, with jobs and all. If they're important. Hey, how much trouble did you get in for the piss bombs?"

I said, "My dad didn't think it was any big deal. Why? What did your dad do?"

Toshi rubbed absently at his wrist. It was a weird habit he'd picked up, as if he'd tricked himself into believing in the ache of a bone that really had snapped and healed. "He yelled at me a bunch. He was pretty mad, saying that I ruined my future. I'm still grounded right now, but tonight is the night he spends with his girlfriend, so he'll never know that I didn't lock myself in my room right after school. Hey, did you hear what Jay's dad did to him?"

I shook my head.

"Dis*owned* him. Right as soon as he walked in the door, dropped him just like that."

"Yikes," I said. "He told you?" I didn't say, Jay forgot to tell that to me. Jay was supposed to tell me everything, and whenever Toshi let out a tidbit I didn't know, I prickled with jealousy.

"It only lasted two days, though. Jay did a bunch of groveling or made promises or something so that his dad would let him back in. He wasn't going to be allowed on this Kentucky trip, but he convinced his dad that he needed the discipline of the conference, or something like that, and then his dad must have realized it would be better to take him along than leave him home alone for the weekend." Toshi nodded. "So he got to go."

Jay must have been miserable for those days he was disowned, but I hadn't even noticed, preoccupied as I'd been with my own concerns. It was funny because I might not even notice if my father disowned me, a punishment he'd probably never think up in the first place. You couldn't disown something that barely seemed like yours.

A car drove past us; the kids inside yelled, "Dickwads!" and threw a half-empty milkshake that splattered across my shins. Our big reveal as the piss bombers hadn't made us popular at school; instead, everyone seemed to hate us more. "Let's get out of here," I said.

Toshi stared up at the sky. "My dad locked away my stereo and all my magazines and books and horn because of the whole piss bomb thing. My room is like a jail cell, now. I think maybe I'll stay in New Veronia tonight, even though I might catch a cold."

Ever since I'd learned about moving to Florida, my house had seemed emptier and emptier, too. When I biked back home, the windows would be black as rats' eyes.

"Yeah," I said, "same here." New Veronia always looked so cozy, sort of like a cabin in a fairy tale, and really, there was no reason for us to go home.

The howling reached me about a hundred paces out from the encampment. Toshi heard it, too: he stopped and sort of hid behind me.

"What *is* that?" he whispered.

"Must be the Zimzee," I said, trying for jokey to cover up the fact that I was scared.

Another howl, more pitiful sounding than the first, wafted among the trees. I picked up a branch and held it like a baseball bat as we made our cautious way into New Veronia. Maybe Mark had discovered our fort and he was trying to scare us as revenge for that night at the party.

But what we found in New Veronia was a dog: her back left paw had been caught by our bear trap. She snarled when she saw us, but I could tell that she only hated us because she was terrified. She'd chewed up her leg—bits of red flesh dangled from it—and her foot angled unnaturally on the other side of the trap.

"I thought those things didn't work," I said.

Toshi shrugged. "Jay lubed them up after that time they didn't go off."

After that time they didn't snap closed on my father, he meant.

The dog was so skinny that her heavy panting racked her whole body—all her bones were shaking. "Do you think there was just a little scrap more of meat over there, and she sniffed it out?"

"Maybe," Toshi said. "Or Jay might have baited it again. We have to put her out of her misery."

I wanted to tell Toshi that no, we could let her go, maybe she'd heal up, but of course I knew that she never would. Besides, if we tried to get close enough to free her, she'd bite us, for sure. "Don't you wish Jay was here? He could use his gun."

"We'll have to do it." Toshi walked around behind New Veronia—a bunch of old tools were rusting against the north side of the triplex, things we had borrowed from our fathers and never returned, not that they had noticed—and came back with a shovel.

I stared at him, shocked. "Isn't there anything quicker?" I couldn't believe that hypochondriac, pee-shy Toshi was prepared to bludgeon a dog to death, but I was also grateful that he wasn't asking me to do it.

"It's better this way. Even if she wants to keep on living, she shouldn't."

I distracted her for the first blow so that Toshi could sneak up behind and get her good, but then I had to look away; it took a long time. I helped Toshi dig the grave, though.

After we'd finished, we scuffed around the grounds of New Veronia and talked lethargically about making improvements. We'd dragged an old toilet behind some bushes, but it didn't have a pipe to convey away the waste, and we mostly just peed against trees. We'd extended the flagpole with the help of a sapling, and now from the ground, the penises Jay had drawn on the flag all those months ago just made it look kind of dirty.

By the time the sky had blackened, I'd regained my appetite. "Let's look in Jay's side to see if there's anything to eat," I said.

"He wouldn't want us going in there with him gone. But there's got to be food in his house. I'm sure there's a window we can climb through or something."

Before we left, Toshi watched silently as I sprung the rest of the bear traps—each one snapped off a few inches of my branch—then covered them up with leaves and sticks so that Jay wouldn't notice the change.

The moon shone brightly enough that we could halfway see where we were stepping in the woods. Without any lights on inside, Jay's house looked abandoned, and the mess of debris around its yard magnified this impression. The window above the kitchen sink hadn't been locked, and we easily slid it open and slithered through, the only mishap being that I placed my foot in a teetering stack of dirty dishes. They toppled with a clash, which set my heart on fire, but of course, no one was home to be disturbed.

Toshi found a grocery bag, and he filled it with beer nuts and those packaged Danishes that had expiration dates months and months into the future. I checked in the fridge, but when I saw a greenish-looking jar of mayonnaise, I shut it quickly.

"Maybe we should go in his parents' room," I said. Jay had never let us in there; since he'd been little, his parents had instilled in him a strong off-limits rule for their part of the house.

"Oh, yes," Toshi said. "Totally. I bet they have a sex swing. Or maybe the place is booby trapped and we'll get our legs lasered off."

My real motive for moving us upstairs was Stella's bedroom and all the wonderful things her body did inside of it, like sleep and get dressed and paint her toenails and dance around to No Doubt—her favorite band. This was my chance: Stella's heavenly room hovered just above my head. As soon as I could ditch Tosh, I'd go there.

Now that Jay's house was empty, it held only a fraction of the fear that it held when there was a chance his parents could return to it at any moment. I walked down the hallway towards Jay's parents' room with my chest held out; I let my footsteps fall loudly, when normally, I would have moved as quietly as possible, listening for any sound. Toshi tiptoed behind me. Stella's room called to me from the opposite direction; I would go there—alone—as soon as I could.

I half-expected the parents' door to be locked—then our mission would be aborted and I could pursue my own course —but instead, the door stood open a few inches. Toshi crowded me as I pushed inside and flipped on the light.

The first thing I noticed was the bed, unmade, with the sheets and blankets twisted up. It shocked me that a bed a woman slept in could look so filthy. The comforter was printed with a confederate flag, and the sheets were stained. The room smelled dank and close, with undertones of hair gel and, probably, sex. This heady rush of déjà vu overtook me, but I couldn't place it: I'd never been here before. It was probably just that I had imagined this room, or maybe it was the smell, the same mix of scents you might find in any couple's room. Stella's room would smell of sugar and coconut sunscreen.

Mounted on the wall over the bed was a rack holding three shotguns, and parallel to that a few knives were tacked up like photos of beloved ancestors. On a dresser, tilted among bottles of lotion, combs, deodorant, and oozing tubes, stood a framed picture of Jay's parents on what must have been their wedding day. They both wore white; both of them had long, straight hair framing their long faces. The resemblance between Stella and her mom was strongest around the chin, which came to a pretty, narrow point in both women.

"Why do you think they don't let anyone in here?" Toshi asked as he opened drawers in the bedside table. "Condoms, maybe? We should get some of those. Or sex toys?"

I was looking over Toshi's shoulder when he lifted up a bible that was holding down a stash of porn magazines. Probably Jay's dad only liked the bible for its quotes like "There were their breasts pressed, and there they bruised the teats of their virginity." Or more likely he didn't read it at all.

"Jackpot," Toshi said. He eased out the bottommost magazine and dropped it into the plastic grocery bag that held our rations for the night. There were a few crumpled tissues in the drawer, too, and he plucked off one that had stuck to the corner of the magazine. "It's probably covered in germs." He headed into the master bathroom and began to wash his hands.

"You find any condoms?" I said. "Married people probably don't use them, anyway."

"Or they took them on vacation. People do it a lot when they're on vacation." Toshi, air drying his hands, pushed the bedside drawer closed with his foot. The noise of its slam should have been expected, but we both jumped. He bent to search under the bed. "Look what I found." He held the little tube beneath my nose. "Lube!"

"Huh," I said. My déjà vu had started to devolve into revulsion; the smell of sweat and aerosol choked me. I needed to get out of there. For some reason, I hated that room.

"I wonder if it makes dick taste like dick, or like strawberry." He unscrewed the cap and sniffed.

My chest was being squeezed by a giant hand. "I'm going to go take a piss," I said as Toshi touched a teardrop of lube to his tongue.

"Strawberry," he said and laughed. "Chicks really do love that flavor."

I zipped out of there and stood for a moment in the hallway, panting. Then I headed straight for Stella's room. The door pushed open over a pile of skirts and tank tops, and I inhaled deeply, already feeling tingly. Posters of Nick Carter and kittens, both with lipstick marks on them, covered one wall, and a bulletin board crammed with junk like old invitations, dance flyers, and coupons covered another. No Doubt CDs were propped on the windowsill.

In the dirty clothes hamper, I dug down until I found a pair of purple underwear that kind of reminded me of the bikini Stella had been wearing when I'd seen her sunbathing. I stood *here*, in Stella's room, where I'd always longed to be invited. The mirrored closet door perfectly reflected the twin bed, and I wondered if she watched herself while she did stuff on the mattress. Or maybe she watched whatever guy was with her—but no, her room was probably pure, because Jay's dad would never let her have a guy in here.

I turned off the light so that no signal would show to Toshi from beneath the closed door. The room became patches of dark and less-dark, which made everything in it seem even more mysterious and important.

Sprawled out on Stella's bed, I inhaled her purple panties. The experience was making me feel better than any porn I'd ever seen, including the internet stuff Toshi and Jay and I had found that first week after Toshi's dad had bought a computer, before he figured out the parental controls.

I closed my eyes and projected images of Stella across their lids. Her bed seemed like the softest thing in the world, but I knew her skin would be softer. Her panties felt slippery against my lips and nose, and I started to get that throb that meant if I didn't come soon, the semen would explode backwards inside of me and give me a bellyache. I unzipped.

When I heard the door groan open, I paused only for a moment in my stroking. Though I kept my eyes closed, I knew that Toshi had found me. Maybe if I didn't look at him, he would go away. Maybe he couldn't see me through the shadows. I'd never masturbated with anyone else in the room; I'd never done anything with another human being, and so it was a shock when he touched me, but it was also like I'd been teetering on the edge of a cliff for years and finally, finally, someone had pushed me off.

I was laid out on Stella's sheets; I was with Stella; it was so easy to pretend that Toshi was her. Stella with her round tits and her high little butt and her soft, warm mouth that suddenly wrapped itself around my tip.

All five of my senses were hallucinating: I could smell Stella, I could feel her on me; I heard the brush of her beautiful hair and tasted her pussy. Behind my closed eyes, I saw her; it was *her* getting me off. My head pressed back into Stella's pillow as the tingling sensation traveled down my thighs, up my torso, and through my brain in waves. It was fantastic, it was fucking Stella, it was bizarre as my penis grew and grew and took over the entire atmosphere, conducting the very air into vibrations of pleasure.

I think that Toshi was touching himself as he sucked me, and I think he swallowed my load, too, but like I said, I never looked at him, not once the whole time, so I wouldn't know. After I finished, he stood up and then I heard him moving around downstairs. He must have left out the kitchen window, but I wanted to make sure he was gone before I did the same, so I jerked off two more times, but the feeling was more hungry and raw, not as all-encompassing as the first time.

I didn't feel gay, not one bit, because I'd wanted it to be Stella doing those things to me; I'd pretended that it *was* Stella so hard that basically, it had been.

All this whacking off must have exhausted me, because I woke up in the morning in Stella's bed. Toshi wasn't around. I tried to think that I had dreamed the whole thing, and Toshi hadn't been there at all, but it was impossible to trick myself that way. I knew that we'd never talk about what had happened between us.

I put everything back in its place—everything but Stella's panties—so that no one would know we'd been there, and as soon as I closed the kitchen window behind me, I wished fiercely that I could burn that whole house to the ground.

Chapter 12

I skipped school the day after our break in, a Friday—I just didn't go, I told myself that I wouldn't and I didn't, and no consequence came of it—and so I didn't see Toshi again until Monday. Jay had returned by then, which made our dynamic feel regular, the same-old same-old, except for that, sometimes, when I looked at Toshi, I worried that I was only my cock, that my cock was me, that it owned me. This was a concern I'd had before: in class, at the most inconvenient of moments, my cock would demand all of my brainpower, it would force me to think about Stella's thighs, so that I'd miss a whole lesson. Or I'd have to hurry off to the bathroom, part-ways crouched.

That Monday at lunch, I asked Jay about his trip.

"Oh, man. It was great." Jay pushed aside his food to talk, which I had never seen him do before. "I feel like I have a real action plan for life now. A real direction. Everybody there was so *into* it. Me and my dad, we went to all these sessions together; we really figured out some shit."

"Did you meet any girls?" I asked.

"What do you mean, an action plan?" Toshi said. "What are you going to do?"

"There weren't girls there; they were women. You should have *seen* these women. Dressed up in skirts and shit. Tweed. I never thought that a bun was a sexy hairdo, but now I know different. You got to dress superior if you are superior. You can really tell who's who, just from their outfit."

"I'm all about buns," I said. "You get with any of them?"

"It wasn't that kind of meeting. We were doing real work." Jay started eating again. "But it was so weird." He spoke with his mouth full. "When we got back, my parents were sure that someone had broken into our house, but they didn't steal anything."

I ducked my head to hide my surprise. How could they have possibly figured out that we'd been in their house? It was messy to begin with, and we'd left everything exactly as we'd found it—almost. It seemed impossible that they could have noticed anything off. "Do they"—my voice squeaked, so I started again—"do they have any idea who it might be? I mean, what would they do to someone like that? A burglar?"

"The crime around here keeps growing and growing," Toshi said. "I'm surprised you haven't been broken into before. Just last month, nonviolent crimes in Delaware rose by three percent."

Jay said, "We're ready if the asshole tries it again. That's one thing this conference got us: is ready. Speaking of—Janet is all set to come to New Veronia this weekend, Sunday, she likes to do it after church or whatever, so you two coxos need to find your girls *now*. Go into serious survivalist mode. Hunt twenty four-seven until you trap one. It's the kill that matters."

My heart flipped up into my mouth—Jay had just called us cock suckers—and I had to force it back down again. He said coxos all the time, but it wasn't literal. Once I'd recovered, I said, "Does Janet have a sister or someone, maybe?"

"Quit dreaming."

The lunchroom din made my body feel like a hundred

little weights were strapped to it, and my blood quickened even before I looked behind my shoulder and saw—a miracle —Stella eating alone. I felt like I was in a trance as I stood up and floated my way over to her. Ever since we'd started school, my eyes had been constantly sweeping the merchandise, rotating over bodies in class, in the hallways, in the cafeteria. But really, though I would have gladly taken basically anyone who wanted me, the only girl I wanted was Stella.

"Hey," I said, sitting down next to her in the mystifyingly empty seat.

She glanced up at me, but said nothing. While I searched for a witticism or a compliment, I nervously picked up a forgotten spork. Its tines were tiny, ineffective, and I snapped one of them off. The triangle of it in my palm looked like a cartoon eyelash. My mother had shaped her eyelashes into spikes with black wax. Whenever my mother had cried, dark rivulets had flowed down her face. Back then, I'd figured that her tears were different from my father's, that men's and women's tears looked different, that tears were just another physical variance between the sexes. Kids are so stupid.

"So," I said finally, feeling massively discouraged. "How are classes going? Did you hear about that pop quiz in history? Mr. Ollsen is trying to crush us, but all the kids who had history first period warned us about it."

"I'm not an idiot." One of her pretty shoulders lifted and then fell.

"You're probably the smartest girl I know." I started to worry that she was acting so prickly because she'd smelled me in her room, on her pillow, or she'd found one of my hairs on her floor, or she sensed that I'd already had sex with her in my mind. Or maybe she'd missed her purple panties —I pressed a hand over my front right pocket, where I'd been transferring them every morning when I got dressed; they were still there, deep down.

"What do you want?" she said. I had the feeling that her

eyes were shifting around, trying to gauge how many people at school were noticing us together, though she stared only at the juice box in front of her.

I pushed on. "Me and Toshi and Jay, we've been working in the woods, I mean, you know, we built this really killer thing, actually, and we're having this… party, a small sort of party, this weekend, Sunday, and I was wondering if maybe you would like to come as my date?"

"*Date?*"

I clenched my hands together and tried to smile.

"Do you still think that people *do* that? Go on actual dates? My god."

"Maybe you'll have fun?" I said, my voice way too small.

"Go on a *date?* And my *brother* is there?"

"You wouldn't have to be around him, not hardly at all, because you would be mostly with me. There's a place for us to… we could have privacy."

"What are you always *doing* around him?"

"Who?"

"Jay. He's getting worse. Like when he got that stupid tattoo, and he thought it made him a man."

When Jay showed up one day with a tattoo at just thirteen years old, we'd all been impressed. A tattoo on the back of his neck, where it was clearly visible, *did* seem like the mark of an adult.

"He's really buying into this whole thing of our parents. Maybe it's because he doesn't have soccer to wear him out anymore. Our dad is such a tool, but Jay wants him to be proud, and now Jay's whipped. You should see the way they talk to each other, like they're in the military when really they're just in the kitchen drinking juice."

Several tables away, Jay was holding a fist over Toshi's unopened milk container. I said, "What do you mean, the whole thing of your parents?"

Stella rolled her eyes. "Their white culture stuff. Like… skinheads."

The noise and activity of the cafeteria whirled around me, and I felt like I was at the center of a giant wheel, with everything but me on the move. "Like, kind of racist?"

"You should have *seen* some of the people at this conference. I can't believe they made me go."

Jay wasn't a skinhead; he had a crew cut. "I don't know what you're talking about. One of his best friends isn't white. Toshi." Jay and Stella hated each other in the way that seemed typical of siblings, so I couldn't fault her for making her own family sound like creepy skinheads, but she didn't really know Jay; I knew Jay, and he was a great guy, my best friend.

Stella said, "He loved that crazy conference. He went to every session. Meanwhile, I was stuck there in Ken*tuck*y and my boyfriend decides to hook up with Lucy. One weekend away, and that's what I get. Are guys really that desperate?"

"Lucy's not so great." She had a big rack and she was rich, one of the only kids at school to own a cell phone, but her voice was dog-whistle annoying and everyone called her Double- O Loosey because of how much she got around.

"Probably I should have caved in and slept with him," Stella said.

If she was lying, her face didn't give it away. Maybe Jay had misunderstood what his sister was out doing with guys, or maybe she was pretending to be a prude. "Well," I said, "I'm glad you're single."

"You don't really care," she said. "Stop pretending like you want anything more than to have sex with me. I see the way you look at me. It's gross."

My eyes felt dried out from staring at her in shock. It wasn't that Stella hated me, it was that she had me all wrong; she thought I was like every other asshole. Finally I got my jaw to work. "What I feel, it's deeper than that, it's got a history, I've felt this way for years, now…"

"Whatever," Stella said. "Jay told me how you really are."

"I'm not!" My voice squeaked. "He was just joshing. You know how Jay is. Right?" I couldn't believe that Jay was trying to sabotage my chance with Stella. I rambled on, trying to hit on an eloquent speech about why Stella needed to come with me to New Veronia— but in the end, all I could manage was, "So we're on for this Sunday? It's a date?"

Her mouth tightened up in a smile; I felt ready to kiss her right then. "Hey!" Stella was shouting across the cafeteria at a girl she always hung around with. "This guy wants me to go on a *date* with him!" Then she burst into hysterical laughter.

One of the worst parts, besides the entire cafeteria looking at me as if I were an idiot, was that Stella hadn't said my name; to her, I was just *this guy*, when I thought about her name maybe fifty times a day.

As I stood up and walked stiffly towards the bathroom, the only place I could be almost pretty much alone at school, Stella said, "Don't be such a dork about everything." And then she returned to eating her lunch.

Locked inside of a stall, the stench didn't even bother me; it was like the sense of smell had been burned right out of my face from shame.

"Soppy?" some asshole said over the din of his piss splashing into the urinal. "Is that you hiding out in here? Oh Sops, that only makes us all think worse of you."

I waited until the bathroom was empty again to scream into my cupped hands. The hot moisture of my breath collected against my palms, and a yellow glob of spittle lodged between my fingers. My body seemed made up of pus, like I was rotting from the inside, as if puberty—what a stupid word—was dissolving and then replacing me with a gooey alien.

When I'd pulled myself together enough to return to my table, I got out my history book and buried my face inside of it, trying frantically to memorize facts for the pop quiz. Studying was the perfect excuse to keep me from looking like I was about to die of misery.

"Bennet." Jay rapped a knuckle against my head. "Are you listening? I never got what you saw in her." Jay glanced over at his sister. "She has bacne."

"I'll get a girl for this weekend," I said. "But sometimes there are more immediate concerns."

"I don't think so," Jay said. "Why am I surrounded by such losers? The only reason to go to this shitty school is to be around girls. Now that I can't do soccer." Jay stared broodingly at the soccer team's table. When I followed his gaze, it struck me that the kid he'd peed on in the shower, the freshman, was black. I shook my head hard: but that wasn't the reason Jay hated him. The reason was because he'd made varsity by being someone's little brother.

"He has a history test." Toshi pointed to my textbook.

"What does it matter?" Jay said, and something snapped in my brain: it was like the final puzzle piece landing home so that I could see the whole picture, and I finally understood what was important.

I flipped the textbook shut. "How do they get us to care about this stuff, anyway?" I said. "When it's true: we should care about the pussy. That's what we should worry about." The only reason I tried so hard in school was because I wanted to skip ahead into the smart classes with Stella, but somehow I hadn't realized until Stella had called me a dork that all the guys she dated were practically failing out. She didn't care if I was smart; in fact, being smart detracted from my attractiveness.

"But you've always gotten good grades." Toshi nudged

the history book towards me. "I mean, you kind of care about that stuff—you know?"

"He's finally waking up," Jay said. "Finally understanding what the world *is*."

It was true that I got okay grades—B's, mostly—and that Jay and Toshi got C's and some D's (except in English, where Toshi aced everything), but my grades had done nothing besides keep me from taking classes with my friends and fuel my stupid reputation as an undesirable nerd. All of a sudden, the sight of my history book made me feel devastated for all the hours lost, all the lost hours I'd spent cramming facts and completing homework and filling out flash cards; all that time had done nothing for me. I couldn't even remember the dates and formulas I'd memorized before the summer.

"No, Toshi," I said, "I'm not going to study anymore. Jay's right: it doesn't do me any good. Don't look all disappointed. Damn. It's not like I could ever afford to go to college."

Toshi's eyes flickered; they never met mine. This was the worst part about what had happened: before Stella's room, we used to be just friends, but now there was this covert rift between us.

Next period, in theater, I had my monologue test. As Mr. Blake held a pen over a clipboard, I stood in front of the class and began.

" 'No more—and by a sleep to say we end/The heartache, and the thousand natural shocks/That flesh is heir to.' " When Stella had thrown me that look of disgust in the cafeteria, the world had started to spin a little too fast. Everything was changing, and each adjustment was a tick closer to a completely unfamiliar and frightening existence, maybe sort of like the place where Hamlet lived, a kingdom of death and madness and despair made worse by his disloyal mother. The remainder of Shakespeare's lines fled from my tongue. I opened my mouth, but my monologue was over.

"You didn't get very far with the words," Mr. Blake said, "but that emotional display was brilliant. Fantastic change from last year. Real tears out of a young man like you! Can you cry on cue all of the time?"

"Bathroom," I mumbled as I headed for the door.

I wandered the hallways and pretended that I was in a strange zoo: each classroom I passed, I would look through the narrow glass window at the humans trapped inside. When I came to the music room, I heard the band practicing the fight song. Someone—a flute, it sounded like—was a half-beat behind everyone else. Through the window, I saw Toshi puffing on his horn, his cheeks distended. Quickly, I looked away, fighting against a twinge of revulsion. The hallway stretched long and silent and empty and sterile: maybe I was the one on the wrong side of the doors; maybe I was the one trapped.

Chapter 13

That Saturday, the sky turned from cloudy to sun-filled in the middle of the afternoon. My dad slammed the door when he came in, and then he knocked against the couch, which had been in the same place forever. He'd probably been drinking for days, or weeks; we hadn't done anything together—we'd hardly spoken—since he'd told me the news about my mother. All of a sudden, as he stepped too-precisely around the coffee table, a well of anger opened up in me over this neglect.

I stood between him and the refrigerator, which was filled with beers. Somehow, he always knew exactly how many he had left: if he hadn't, I would have taken some for me and Jay. "Are you drunk?" I asked.

"Of course not." He rubbed at his forehead. "Why are you always home?"

"It's two o'clock in the afternoon."

He pushed me away from in front of the fridge so that he could get a Sam Adams.

"Don't *touch* me," I said.

He looked through me for a second, and then he turned away. Now that he was sending me off to my mom, I'd become invisible to him. I wondered if he'd been acting like this when my mom decided to leave the family. If I were his wife, it would have pissed me off, but since I was his son, it mostly let me do what I wanted. And what I wanted right then was to yell at him. "You're so *stupid*," I said. "No wonder Mom got out of here."

He drank calmly, his neck bobbing, and then said, "If you want the truth, Stacey was like a flash of lightning." He waved his hands around, spilling a little from the bottle. "She won't stick to things—just lights them up for a second."

My mother's first name had basically slipped from my vocabulary, and so it was strange to hear it coming out of my father's mouth.

"She uses fate to get out of things," he said. "This religious kind of fated future that lets her pretend nothing she does matters. You don't know how she is."

The room smelled like dry, crushed leaves and alcohol sweat, and I hated the sun for coming in through the blinds to illuminate the mess of our lives.

"What she decided had nothing to do with me. *I* wasn't the one who changed." He blinked rapidly.

"It wasn't my fault," I said. "I was a *baby*."

"Benny, don't cry. I wanted a son so bad. You'll be fine with your mom."

"I'm not crying. Why does everybody keep saying that?"

"She's ready to see you. And then you and me, we can have a little breathing room from each other. It will be good."

I had this crazy idea like maybe my dad was so desperate to get away from me that he'd coerced some random woman into pretending to be my mother: it wasn't like I would be able to tell the difference, not if he found a good actress. Or maybe this really was his way to give me a relationship with my mother, and there was a chance that things with her would turn out okay, that we would have a moment together like that final scene in *The Importance of Being Earnest*, when all the confusion melts away and we finally understand each other's truths and all obstacles to love are overcome.

Just joshing.

"So you wanted me back then," I said, "but you don't want me now."

He pulled at the beer. "I guess the truth is, you changed." My dad shrugged as if to say that I'd become inexplicable, and I had to admit that I knew how he felt: sometimes, I seemed like a stranger from myself; it wasn't fair that my dad could escape me, but I never could.

He said, "Teenagers are different than babies."

I looked down at my arms, at the hair growing out of them that seemed to darken with each day. Fathers were the worst. Even if he plugged me in the face, I wouldn't be able to feel any more terrible. Anything bad that happened to me from now on would be his fault because he'd given me up. "I'm sick of you. I'm glad I'm getting away."

Finally he looked up and straight into my eyes. "Okay. It's for the best."

I hated him, I hated him, I hated him.

———

On Sunday, I met Toshi and Jay in New Veronia; the girls were supposed to show up right around six. Since Stella had turned me down so publicly, I'd asked Jessica, a freshman who lived a couple blocks from my house; Charlene, who sat beside me in math; and Danni, just because I'd run into her —literally, I'd jammed her with my book—in the hallway, but her visible bra straps had made me so nervous that I wasn't even sure she'd been able to understand all the details of the invitation through my stammer.

The three of us shuffled around New Veronia, tossing sticks out of the clearing, checking the toilet, straightening our mattresses. Inside my room, I hung a pillowcase over the spot where I'd carved Stella's name into the wood. I'd thought for sure she'd visit me there and think it was romantic.

When walking past the door to Jay's room, I caught sight of the fluffy gray plume of Dave the squirrel's tail. I started to head over to see if I could get Dave to chatter at me the way he sometimes did when he was in a conversational mood, and it took me several seconds to realize that Dave was dead.

"What the hell happened to Dave?" I said to Jay as I strode up, fast, to the log where he sat surrounded by whittled shavings.

Jay didn't look up from the stick he was forming into a point. "Shot him."

"Squirrels breed disease," Toshi called from his spot beneath a tree.

"You shot Dave and nailed him above your door?" I could feel my features puckering around my nose, which made me look like a wuss, but I couldn't help it.

Jay shrugged. "Looks neat. Besides, you can't be sure that one was Dave. They're all the same."

I thought about prying down Dave and giving him a proper burial, maybe next to the dog that Toshi had killed, but I didn't want to get dead squirrel smell all over my hands before the girls came, so instead I climbed up a tree just far enough to peek over the leaves to the blue suggestion of bay miles and miles away.

Six o'clock arrived with us three feeling a little wild from the anticipation, and I tried to draw Jessica, Charlene, and Danni closer with thought, sort of a kinetic exercise, but after a couple of hours had passed and still no girls had arrived, we started to realize that we'd been stood up, all of us, even Jay. Because I wasn't the only one, I didn't feel so much like dying of humiliation.

"What the fuck." Jay kicked at the ground, sending up a spray of earth. "Those fucking bitches. Think they can do this to us."

"Maybe they got lost," Toshi said.

"No. I drew a map. We would have heard them yelling or giggling or something if they were out there. Soppy, this is your fault; you didn't get the strawberry wine coolers."

After the long, disappointing wait, I felt tight, like the chains of a swing that had been spun around and around. "Why do you people always call me that?" I asked. "It's really not even funny. It doesn't make any sense."

Jay and Toshi exchanged a puzzled look. "*You* know why," Jay said.

But I didn't. I had no idea. All I knew was that Soppy had followed me through every grade since I'd moved to Delaware, it had been the access point for everyone to pick away at me, to keep me out, to bring me down. I *hated* Soppy. I grabbed a stick and stabbed at the ground between my feet, trying to unwind myself. "Why did you say that to Stella?" I asked Jay, the thing I'd been wanting to ask him all day. "You told her that I'm just trying to get in her pants?"

"It's true." Jay shrugged. "I know you invited her out here. Even though I told you not to. And there's only one reason we built this whole place."

I wanted to explain how I was connected to Stella on a level deeper than sex, how our conversations in the last few days had changed my life, had put me on a new trajectory, had let me see the truth about school, but I knew Jay wouldn't get it. Anything heartfelt inspired his scorn. I said, "You've never wanted me to be with her. Probably it's you who's been sabotaging our relationship from the start."

"You don't got a relationship," Jay said.

"But we could have," I said. "If you didn't stick your fat lies into it."

"At least I got something fat for the sticking."

I fell into a seething silence, and the others didn't talk, either. In the quiet, there was nothing, no giggles, no faint whiff of candy perfume. Dark had taken over by now; everything felt still and shut down.

"I have an idea," Jay said. "We don't need these stupid girls. Virgins, ain't they? They don't know how to do it."

None of us brought up the fact that we were virgins, too.

"What if we get a real woman? I mean, one who does this for a living? Women sell their bodies all the time, if you go to the right place. We just need to get over there."

"We don't have any money," Toshi said. "How much would she want? For us to... how much does that cost, anyway? It has to be a lot."

"I don't have any money," I said. "Maybe... ten dollars is all." I was still hoarding the bill my father had given me.

"Oh, god. Oh, Jesus. You two are idiots. Think about how it works: she has sex with you, *then* she gets paid. If there's no money, there's no money. You've already got the goods. Get it?"

Something about the clear, dark night, the horniness of waiting for a girl who never came—even though I knew that Jessica, Charlene, and Danni were just about as likely to show up as Stella or that TV actress with huge tits I jerked off to sometimes—and the way Jay always sounded like an expert, made his idea seem pretty smart. Besides, since the fight with my dad, I was feeling desperate for something good. I was ready to try anything: I deserved this. We had worked all summer on New Veronia, and so I deserved this now.

"Okay," I said. "But where are these women? And how do we get to them?"

"We only need to get to one of them," Jay said, "because one will do all of us."

My eyes were opened as wide as they could go in the dark, but still I couldn't see any better.

"We'll take my dad's truck. Okay? He'll never notice that it's gone. They're going to go to sleep soon, anyhow; we'll wait until then."

"But," Toshi said, "aren't you worried that your dad will find out about you always taking his truck?"

"No way, I mean, he already found out. He knows about the truck. He's there for me; he understands sometimes I got to do what I got to do. He knows I take it when I really need it."

"Huh." Toshi looked down at his feet with a sort of disappointed expression, and I wondered if he was realizing the same thing I was: we had nothing on Jay; we'd never have anything to hold over Jay's head. The guy was basically invincible, and I admired him for that.

We all piled into Jay's portion of the triplex to finesse our plan. He turned on the camping lantern he'd brought from his garage and pulled out some paper and a pencil. He had a lot of stuff in his New Veronia room, much more than Toshi or me; it was as if he'd slowly been transferring his bedroom out of his parents' house.

"First," Jay said, his pencil poised over the paper, "let's try to visualize this bitch." He drew a circle for her head with long strands of hair coming down on either side. Her eyes were two more circles with spidery lashes and her mouth was an empty O. Each of her Venn diagram breasts were bigger than her head, and they had little stick arms and legs coming off of them.

"Hm," I said. "Appealing." I meant to sound funny, but the blank face creeped me out.

"That's a sexy woman." Jay punctuated this sentence with a stab of the pencil point between her eyes.

Finally, it was late enough. Outside, the night air felt warm as a bath, and excitement had caffeine-frizzled my nerves. "Do you know where we're going?" I asked Jay as he had us pile into the pickup truck.

"Absofuckinglutely. I been there before."

Toshi shifted in the middle bench seat. "Oh yeah? When?"

"My dad, he's driven me by the red light district. Not like we did anything. We yelled at the whores, is all, called them sluts and whatever. Once you have a wife, they don't matter for nothing, but until then, I guess they're a pretty doable option."

On the drive there, the swaying cab grew overfull with the smells of sweat and cologne. I asked Jay if we should have brushed our teeth, if we should stop and rinse out our mouths, but he said, "It doesn't matter what she thinks. That's the brilliant thing: I don't know why I didn't think of this before. It doesn't matter what she wants; only what *we* want."

"Well," Toshi said, "*I* don't want to get any kind of disease."

"Think of her as a warm-up." Jay braked too hard at a stop sign. "We're just going to practice on her. Later, we'll get some girls from the high school. Okay? I promise." Jay pulled to the side of the road. "Be right back; I got to piss."

"Maybe this will cheer him up," Toshi said after Jay got out. "Did you hear that his dad was just canned? That means he's around the house all the time, angry. Jay is staying out of his way."

I didn't have a chance to say anything before Jay jumped back inside the cab.

When we got to the street that Jay called the red light district, I saw that there weren't any red lights at all. It was a trash-strewn, narrow road behind the WalMart.

"Here it is," Jay said, revolving his hands on the wheel. I knew that his palms were sweating because of the way they squeaked against the rubber.

"Where are the girls?" Toshi said. All that shone in the headlights was a clogged gutter and a broken-up sidewalk.

"Give them a minute to get off their asses," Jay said, "and then we'll drive through, nice and slow. Keep your eye out for the one you want. A white one; big tits."

I felt like I was in a movie: important, rich, playing someone else. We'd find a woman as voluptuous and sex-crazed as those from the magazine underneath the bible in Jay's parents' room, and then she'd get in the car with all three of us, and we'd have turns at wild sex with her. Finally, instead of pay, we'd zoom away, our jizz the only thing she'd get out of the encounter. She'd yell some dirty words after our retreating tail lights, but she'd never be able to find us again. Forever after, she'd play a role in my wet dreams.

"My dad showed me this porno once," Jay said, "so that I could see the differences. There are real differences between the white ones and the black ones."

"Your dad watched porn with you?" Toshi said.

"It was educational: the black ones want it all the time and so there's more of a chance you might catch something from them. Plus, their asses are like, denser."

"Huh," Toshi said. I stayed silent, feeling buzzed about

what we were going to do. Jay gently stepped on the gas and the truck began its rumbling path down the road.

A few bodies had stepped out from the shadows, or maybe they had been there, and only now were the headlights picking them up. There were legs in sheer black stockings, skinny legs, mostly, one pair of plump legs; long hair gleaming unnaturally, as if it held light within it; eyes done up so that they were black circles in the face. These were not exactly the prostitutes of television; I don't know why I kept expecting the world to be like television: any resemblance had been disproven often enough.

"That one has huge tits," Jay said.

"But maybe they would smother you." Toshi rounded both his hands in front of his face. "Too much, you know?"

"Don't roll down the window," Jay said, "until we find the one we want."

I think we all must have seen her at the same time. Actually, she looked sort of like Jay's mother, but without the severe hairdo, with more makeup to soften her features. She had medium-sized breasts and, after we rolled down the window, I saw that she had large, straight teeth.

"Hey, boys," she said when Jay pulled to the curb. She leaned against the passenger door, inches from me.

"You working?" Jay asked, his voice sounding deep and manly and *knowing*. But he couldn't have done this before; he would have told us, bragged about whatever conquest to no end.

"Are you cops?" she said. "You're too young to be cops. How old are you, anyway?"

"Old enough," Jay said, spiteful-like.

"Ha!" She sucked on her perfect teeth. "Right. You saved up your allowance for this?"

The cherry smell of her bubblegum, or maybe her perfume, had gotten me hard. Her shirt was cut low and I had the perfect vantage straight down it.

"What's your name?" I said. My voice came out soft, but somehow, it still sounded good.

"Destiny," she said and snapped her gum.

"That's pretty." I reached into my pocket and pulled out the ten dollars, all the money I had in the world. "There's more where this came from," I said.

If I had looked over my shoulder at Toshi and Jay, I'm sure they would have seemed impressed, but I couldn't take my eyes from Destiny's. She grabbed the money out of my hand, her fingers touching mine, and I felt that touch in my groin.

The money disappeared below the truck window and she said, "How old are you, anyhow? I can't be doing kids. What if this is a sting operation?"

"I'm driving, ain't I?" Jay said. "We're eighteen, okay? Look, I got a tattoo." He turned so she could see it on the back of his neck. "They won't needle you unless you're of age. Come on, you took his money. Now you got to do something. Then we'll give you more."

"I'm obligated?" Her pretty smile took on a hint of a sneer. "Show me the rest. You don't have to give it to me; just throw it on the dash. For the three of you, hand jobs, I'd need—fifty more."

When she said "hand jobs," I wanted so badly to nuzzle my face against her chest. I wanted to nibble her earlobe so that she could hear me breathing deep inside her head. I needed to pace my breathing, anyhow; I was starting to sound like a train.

"You don't have it," Destiny said. "I can tell."

With that, she turned around, presenting us with her peachy ass in the micro miniskirt, and she walked away from the car.

"You have our ten dollars!" Jay howled. He sounded broken. "Bitch!"

"How did she *know*?" Toshi said. "*How* did she know?"

Destiny must have told all the other women about us, too, because no one else approached our truck. We cruised up and down four times; we would have taken the oldest of them, the one who showed us her empty gums, but even she shooed us away.

"Fuck," Jay said as he drove too fast back to the main road. He slammed a hand against the dash. "Dammit."

"They didn't want the sex," Toshi said. "They only wanted the money. They didn't care about anything else."

"Duh," I said. "Sex is their *job*."

"Why didn't we bring more money? We could have gotten some, somehow." Toshi pressed his legs together in the bitch seat, where he always rode. Cruelly, I thought that he was probably glad we didn't end up with a woman, since he loved to suck cock, and so was basically gay. Unlike me: I'd felt real desire for Destiny.

"Where were we going to get money?" Jay said. "I couldn't get no more money."

"*Any* more money."

"Why are you always correcting his grammar like a faggot?" I said to Toshi.

The cab stayed silent for a moment except for the constant grumble of the tires against the asphalt, and then Jay said, "Yeah, you sound like some old grammar-marm faggot."

Toshi's knees shrunk away from mine; his whole body sort of curled up into itself: a snail. I fought against the urge to apologize, to make him feel better.

But then he said to me, "You're an asshole. I don't care how hard you play dumb: you're the faggot. Not me."

My heart was like a steady hum, it was going so fast. I felt dangerous, my body a haphazard collection of pure energy that could lash out in a hundred directions at once. "Muzzle up." I elbowed Toshi's ribs. "And stop lying."

"Maybe that's why you're getting sent away to Florida," Toshi said. "Because your dad is embarrassed."

Toshi had never been such a bammer to me before, and I wanted to knock the lies right out of him. My eyes felt like they were turning red from the inside out. "That's the dumbest lie I ever heard," I said. "I'm going to see my mom."

"Shut up." Jay parked the car back at his house. "My parents are asleep. Just be quiet until we get back to New Veronia."

Toshi was trying to ruin me by suggesting to Jay that I was gay. There had been a student who transferred to our school in the seventh grade, a guy, but sometimes he'd come to class wearing a skirt, or it would look like he had on mascara, and Jay had hated him. He'd hated the kid so much that, one day after school, he'd followed him home and spray-painted FAGGOT across the kid's house, right there in front of him. Then Jay swore that if the kid told on him, he'd sneak into his bedroom at night and shove a broken bottle up his ass. All this Jay had relayed to me and Toshi with a note of glee in his voice. I couldn't be sure that it had happened just the way Jay told it, but the point was, he took pleasure in telling us, in describing the way he'd carve out the kid's asshole. I knew that he was joking, that it was all one big fantasy to him, but still Toshi had to realize that when he called me a faggot, it was sabotage.

By now, we knew our way through the dark woods; a path had formed from nothing more than our footsteps. Jay brought up the rear, and I felt somehow that he was marching us to a place against our will, though we'd all decided to stay the night in New Veronia already. The triangle of our triplex stood out against the dark-blue sky, and a rib of moon curved just above it.

Once we were inside Jay's room, he declared that our silence could be broken. He switched on the camping lantern and it swung from its ceiling hook, flinging shadows over the walls. I sighed in cautious relief, thinking Jay was going to drop the whole thing, until he said, "Now what was the question, again? The real question? Was it which one of you is a fag?"

"Fuck off," Toshi said, monotone-like. He was slumped across the bed on his back, both his knees pointing to the ceiling. Jay and I stood close to the door.

"It's him," I said. "There's no question: it's him."

"He just might be," Jay said. "I wouldn't put it past him."

The branches of the tree that made up our triplex's center post swished against the tarps. Outside, the wind was picking up.

"And here we've been friends for all these years," Jay said as he stepped closer to the bed, "and I never suspected. Probably he's been spying on me in the bathroom. Or drilled a little peep hole here." He pointed to the wall he shared with Toshi's room.

The wind rushed, and all the cracks in the structure sighed.

"Screw you," Toshi said, trying to sound fierce. He blinked hard. I'd only ever seen him cry one time before, when he got a postcard from Singapore, from his mom, telling him that she got married again. He'd brought the postcard over to my house sealed inside a plastic baggie.

"I was *so* ready to fuck someone tonight," Jay said. The lantern enlarged his shadow, and the dark imprint of him followed as bent over the bed. "And I'm thinking: Toshi wants it."

I pressed my index finger against my thumb, but they were both numb. If Jay turned on me, too, if he somehow knew what Toshi and I had done together in Stella's room, I would die. I would kill myself.

"Don't you want it, Tosh?" Jay put his hands in his belt loops and pulled the fabric of his shorts back against his cock. "It's just to teach you a little lesson. About what it really means to be a faggot."

Toshi had scooted up the bed until his back was against the wall. "Don't touch me," he said.

"We're not going to touch you." Jay stepped closer. "We're just going to fuck you."

In that moment, I realized that Jay was serious.

"Hold on," I said. "Leave him alone. He's our friend, remember? He's not gay."

"Do you want me to fuck you, too?" Jay said to me. "Is that what you're asking for?"

"All I mean is, he didn't do anything." I couldn't keep my eyes on Jay's steely ones.

"That's right," Toshi said. His face was screwed up with fear. "Fuck Bennet, instead. He's gay. He's more gay than me. He made me suck his cock."

The outrage of this statement embodied itself in my hands shaking, and the edges of my vision darkened as if the whole world were tightening its noose.

"What?" I said. "What are you talking about?"

"Oh, my god." Jay was laughing. "This gets better and better. Is he serious? Did you make him suck your cock?"

"No!" I said, over and over again, until I realized that too many denials might make me sound guiltier.

"Well, if he's a faggot lying little shit, then he's asking for it. We have to fuck him."

"Yeah," I said. "Okay. Fuck. Him."

My body felt like the wind outside: everywhere, whipping around, angry. I hated Toshi for what he'd done to me. I hated him most of all for telling Jay, because that meant that I had to prove what Tosh said was wrong. And the only way to do that, Jay had made it clear, was to fuck Toshi.

"Turn him over," Jay said, one knee on the bed. Tosh had curled up in a tight ball, but otherwise, he didn't try to fend me off. When I yanked down his shorts, his ass clenched together, leaving two deep depressions in the muscle on either side.

"I knew I was fucking someone tonight," Jay said.

I watched in fascination as Jay grabbed either of Toshi's cheeks and pried them apart; it was there, that part of a body I'd never much studied, that Jay would fuck. A tight, plummy coil. How would Jay's cock fit in there? Inside my shorts, despite my revulsion, my own cock had started to twitch a little along with the pumping of my heart.

Toshi lay limp, as if we'd killed him first. Jay spat on Toshi's asshole and rubbed the tip of his cock around it. Toshi struggled, his body one quick spasm, and then he lay still as the nighttime bugs started up their chorus.

"He loves it," Jay said, grunting. The shadows beat against the wall. "He loves it, the sick fuck. You got to make sure he can't see your cock." He squashed Toshi's face deeper into the mattress. "Or he'll fall in love with it, the faggot."

This was porn, live: with Toshi face down on the mattress like that, he could pretty much be any woman. I dug in my pocket for Stella's purple panties, then pressed them to my nose and inhaled. They obscured the smell of shit. Maybe my mother had left the family and abandoned me all those years ago because she'd sensed this coming: she had somehow known that I would give in to my wicked body.

"Get in there," Jay said to me, "get in there."

By that point, I would have done anything Jay said; it was like all those years of him being my best friend had embedded his voice in my brain so that his words became my actions. The air on my dick felt strange in the presence of other people. My balls tightened up and it took me a minute to decide that the body on the bed was not Toshi; it was just a body. The wind battered the walls, but I felt nothing of the world outside my own burning anger.

When we had finished and Toshi had pulled his shorts

back up over himself, Jay said, "That *thing* is in my bed. We can't stay here."

"Right," I said, holding fierce onto the last scraps of adrenaline so that I wouldn't feel anything else. The wind flung the door out of my hand and slammed it open. Jay and I stepped out into the night, into a swirl of leaves, and we went whooping through the woods, kids on a sugar high, running and stumbling and fleeing as far from that place as we could.

Chapter 14

We holed up under a tree somewhere surrounded by other trees and, when the adrenaline finally left, it drained every ounce of energy I'd had out with it. As the wind fingered my hair and blew seashell whistles through my ears, I fell into a hard sleep and dreamed that I was in a play, watching a play, which was a dream I'd had before, when I was in theater working on *Midsummer Night's*, and I woke just like the characters, saying *it was all a dream.* They said that to protect themselves, and none of them really believed it.

Then I started itching from bug bites, and though I tried hard to squash the memory, everything came back in too much detail, like the way that Toshi had squealed, the sound reminding me of Podge, the potbelly I'd abandoned in Texas. If only I had been flagged, wasted out of my mind, but a different sort of altered consciousness had made it possible for me to forget that Toshi was my friend, that he was a person and not just a body there beneath me. Maybe it had been a surge of insane hormones or an intense need to prove myself to Jay or a momentary lapse of brainpower: I could only assume that, for those few minutes, my actions had been taken over by something beyond my control. I stuffed my hand into my pocket and rubbed Stella's panties between my fingers.

As soon as Jay opened his eyes, he said, "I'm hungry." He stretched. "Let's get some food."

The trees creaked with their own weight. I wanted to ask if he felt bad or guilty or upset, if his regular expression was just a mask to hide his anguish, but I couldn't talk that way: then it would be obvious that I was shaken up, and maybe changed forever, maybe actually an entirely different person than the one I'd been just yesterday.

Jay found some plants that he said were edible. "My dad taught me how to forage." He snapped the stems of some fern-looking things. "He's kept me out here with him a few nights. Survivalist type stuff."

"You think you could live out here forever? That would be killer." I had to force the enthusiasm into my voice; maybe if I pretended to be myself, I would find me somewhere.

"My dad, you know how he says he's always right, and this one time, I was wondering if he could be wrong just a little. And so"—Jay laughed—"I tried to feed him a bad plant. To see if he was really as smart as he says. If he would notice it. And he did. He did right away. It was only a little joke, but he got pretty mad. Then he left me out for a night all alone for trying to poison him. That was right when there were bears around here, too."

"Wow," I said. "Were you scared?"

"Naw. He'd taught me enough stuff by then."

"Still, that's harsh." I held up the bottom of my shirt to make a basket for our breakfast plants, and Jay dumped them in.

"Come on, that was nothing. I was trying to *poison* him."

"Yeah," I said, though I was thinking that most fathers probably deserved to be poisoned at least a little. "The other day, Stella said this weird thing to me."

"You need to get *over* her. Or I guess if you really want

152

her, then you got to join us. Become a real part of the family."

"That's what I wanted to ask about," I said. "The joining us part. What do you mean, exactly?" Jay did say some messed up stuff, but still it had shocked me when Stella had called her brother a skinhead. In the days since she'd said that, I had been looking at things a little differently, noticing that there were all sorts of signals out there, like graffiti and action films and bumper stickers and stuff the guys said to each other at school. And what we'd done to Toshi—what Jay had convinced me to do to Toshi—I had told myself that Jay couldn't be what Stella had called him, because he had a best friend who was Asian, but the night before, it was like Jay had made Tosh less than human. It had been so easy for me to follow right along.

"All I mean is," Jay said, "if you want to be a part of my family, then be a real part. You got to believe what we believe and do what we do and have the right mindset and all."

"Okay, sure," I said. "And is all that stuff, I mean would you consider it to be, or have you ever called yourself a skinhead?"

Jay snatched up a handful of a bushy-looking plant. "You're thinking about this wrong."

"Okay."

"Did Stella tell you this shit? You have the wrong attitude."

"I didn't know." It was crucial that Jay and I stuck together: we'd done it, we'd kicked Toshi out of our group, we could never be a crew after what had happened—and so we were all each other had left.

" 'Skinhead'—that's not it. That's not it at all. The real name we call ourselves, if you have to know, is the Eye Whites. But 'skinheads' makes you sound like those hate people. Makes you sound like those people who call *us* racist, and then they get all mad when we just want to hang around with our own and mind our own business. If anything, we're race realists, and it's everyone else who thinks they're superior and above all that shit. Like they're so great they can't even see color anymore. We're all about *reality*."

"I just didn't know," I said, my mind turning over that curious phrase *race realists*, still feeling no closer to understanding, but not about to push Jay with more questions.

"You'll figure it out. I'll help you."

"Okay," I said, though I knew Jay wasn't the best at explaining: one time, he'd tried to tell me that they found swastikas on Native American pots from hundreds of years ago, and this proved something about God and purity and the future. He went on and on for half an hour, but I never did understand what he meant.

"It's so obvious that Stella is jealous." Jay ripped up something that looked like a weed, roots and all. "The fact about women is, they only belong to their father's family for a little bit. Then, they go off and belong to their husband's family. So she doesn't get as much attention as me, you know? The family can't put as much into her as they do me." He shook the plant vigorously to dislodge clods of dirt from the roots. "So she gets the wrong idea. Don't listen to her."

Once Jay decided that we had enough plants for breakfast, we sat down. I waited for Jay to eat some green thing before I put the same type of thing into my mouth.

"Sometimes you got to abandon everything else for principles," Jay said. "And in today's world, that is more necessary than ever. I think, for a little while at least, we're on the run."

"On the run? Really?" I tried to tell myself it was the weird green food making my stomach lurch like that, but I felt afraid. Saliva stung the back corners of my mouth. "We didn't…"

"We didn't do anything that bad, no way, but sometimes people get all coxo sensitive. It's stupid. My thought is we let the shit cool down for a little bit. Get out of town for a little bit. Have ourselves an adventure, sort of, while Toshi forgets this whole thing. Besides, there's nothing for us at school, now that I can't play soccer anymore. No point."

I couldn't believe he'd said Toshi's name out loud; I never wanted to say it, not ever again. "But where would we go? How do we get there?"

"You can hitch anywhere," Jay said, "in this great big country of ours. It ain't hard."

Ideas like this were why, throughout our friendship, Jay had always been the visionary. Thank god Jay had known, before I had even realized it myself, the one move that appealed to me: clearing off to a place where nobody knew my name or my social status, knew anything about my dad, where nobody would find out what I'd done to a person I had considered my friend.

"You really think they'd look for us?" I asked Jay. "Like who? The police?"

"Yeah," he said. "Maybe. Tosh is a little wuss, and you can't put it past him to narc."

The decision to just leave, run away, felt unreal, which is maybe why I didn't have that hard of a time making it. This would be one more step in the dream I was having.

"You don't want to go to *jail*," Jay said. "Or juvie, or whatever."

That clinched it for me; it felt so easy to nod my head along. I needed a break from all the madness that had been swirling through my life.

"What about Florida?" I said, swallowing hard on the bitterness of a fern. "I think I can get us somewhere to stay with my mom down there. We'll just go for a little while. Until all this blows over."

Jay spit out a stringy piece of plant stem. "Whatever. Florida sounds far. Just as good as any other place."

━━

After Jay marched up and down the road for maybe a half hour, his thumb stuck out (apparently he wasn't worried about being clipped by a passing side mirror—his movements were loose and a little reckless, and more than once a horn blared as he stepped too close to a car), a little red pickup pulled over and the man inside told us to get in. Jay yanked open the door, and I scrambled after him. Everything was fine: I had been about to head to Florida anyway, and by going now, I would have Jay for support; I wouldn't be leaving everything behind. I was taking matters into my own hands rather than being shipped off to my mother like an unwanted package, like an assortment of old clothes she'd forgotten to pack when she'd left us.

My leaving this way would be the punishment my father deserved.

━━

The driver was bound for somewhere in North Carolina, which was closer to Florida than I had ever been. Incredibly, our plan was really working; I hadn't quite understood there was a possibility we would actually get out of Delaware, that this whole thing wasn't some sort of charade. The asphalt zipping away beneath the floorboards of the truck felt like a miracle, and I pressed myself down into the middle seat to better absorb the vibrations of the road.

"So," the driver said. I'd barely looked at him, and now I was positioned almost too close to his body to get a good view; he smelled of barbecue potato chips and coffee. The pudge of his arm, pink and freckled, sometimes brushed against my shoulder. "You boys are headed to Florida. Land of opportunity?"

"That's right," Jay said. "We got jobs lined up down there."

"Just so long as you're not deserters," the driver said. "I picked you up awfully close to the base, didn't I?"

"We're not deserters, sir," I said; this was a very good sign: to this man, we looked old enough to be eighteen.

"No, sir," Jay said, "I would never run out on something that important."

"Sure." He caressed the wheel. "Sure, is that right. Then you boys don't yet understand this world. You know that? Wouldn't run out on anything important…." The radio devolved into static and he switched it off; on their way back from the dial, the tips of his fingers brushed my knee, which was propped up to a high triangle against the console. I tried to pull myself in tighter.

"Every man runs away," the driver said. "Every man runs away sooner or later. Got it? And it's not our fault. Got it? I ran out on my wife a year, year-and-a-half ago, but it wasn't my fault. We lived by Lewis, had this great townhouse just a couple miles from the beach, had this little girl. Suzie. Had a dog too. All the things. All the family things. Fondue pot."

I started sweating thinking about what he meant by *had* a little girl. Maybe we'd taken up with a cannibal, a kidnapper.

"But it was like providing for my wife made her mad at me. I went to work; she went to help out in the kindergarten room. Cutting out snowmen with safety scissors. Who had the harder job? Her? Or me, slaving away trying to manage a restaurant? Smelling like grease? Rude customers—*I want the booth, I want my dessert comped.*"

Out the passenger side window, the pylon of the bridge dropped a hundred feet into the steel blue water. Tiny boats propelled by tiny men bobbed along the surface, beneath which lurked the fish everyone wanted to haul up. We slowed at the toll booth and then zoomed off as soon as the plastic arm raised.

"Plus, she started accusing me of sleeping around," our driver continued. "With the waitresses, with the bartenders. Those were nobodies. Got it? I love my wife. Ex-wife. I think she was saying that to cover up her fooling with the kindergarten teacher. What kind of sick coupling is that? But I couldn't take it anymore. She kicked me out? I ran off and left her? Who can even remember? Sure, we used to be joined at the hip, me and her."

We pulled over for gas in Virginia, and the man asked us to move to the back of the pickup so that he'd have some room to think. "Going to see her, my ex-wife," he explained, "and I need a real good opening line. Got to figure one out."

I didn't mind the wind-whipped pickup bed; back there, I didn't feel so trapped, plus, it gave me and Jay more freedom to talk.

"You think we can get there in maybe another day?" I said. "This ride you found us is killer." I was starting to feel really good, warm on the outside from the sun and on the inside from heading off on this journey with Jay, who had obviously chosen me over Toshi as his favorite, and even if he'd done that in a way I wanted to forget, the result was the same: Jay and I were on our own adventure.

Jay fished out a candy bar from his backpack. That morning, he'd left me in the woods for what I'd considered an unreasonably long time while he snuck back into his house to gather supplies. He said, "You know that Florida is a great big state, right? Do you got your mom's address? Anything like that?"

"I'll look her up in the book."

The truck flit past billboard after billboard with the same slogan—God Loves Me— all with different people featured, and all defaced in the same way.

Jay paused in munching on his candy bar as we drove through the invisible stench of cows. He said, "Your mom's the perfect one to go to. She'll take us in, and all the way down in Florida, they'll have no clue about the little trouble we got into."

"You think that Toshi told on us?"

Jay threw the candy bar wrapper out of the truck. "Something like that." He shuddered even though the air was pretty warm, and then, pensive and still-bodied in a way I'd never seen him before, he gazed out at the trees. I figured he was finally settling into the guilt of what we'd done.

———

We closed in on North Carolina just before sunset. The driver pulled over and said he was going to leave us there, near to the freeway where we'd have a better chance of getting a ride. "Let me try something out on you boys," he said, "let me test this out." He cleared his throat. "Verna, I know our differences seem pretty big right now, but if you will please accept my sincere apology"—he held out one empty palm—"and this necklace as a token of my true feelings for you"—he held out the other empty palm—"then maybe we can get past... get past the past and move on."

"And then you kiss her," Jay said. "Get right in there for a kiss."

"So it sounds okay? Pretty good, like?"

"I think you have a solid chance," Jay said and hopped out of the pickup.

"Now what should I do if that kindergarten teacher is home?" he said.

"She *lives* with him?" I'd tried to stay out of it the entire ride, but now I'd blown my cover.

"Well yeah." He shrugged. "They're married."

Jay shot me a look that meant I needed to shut my mouth. "You go for it, buddy," he said. "Knock her dead."

After the driver had pulled back onto the road, Jay told me to shoot him if he ever got like that guy, wishy-washy and tied up over a woman, and a *taken* woman at that. "Driving all the way to North Carolina," Jay said, "imagine. She must have been some lay."

Chapter 15

We tried to thumb a ride, but the only car that stopped for us was driven by a black woman, and Jay refused to get in. He waved her on.

"Don't you think she was harmless?" I asked. Her back-seat had looked clean and soft, and I felt desperate for a rest. Standing alongside the on-ramp with all those vehicles screaming past was crumpling up my nerves. "Just an old lady."

"You don't know what she wanted," Jay said. "Could have wanted anything, could have taken us anywhere. It's way suspicious that the old crow even stopped for us in the first place."

"Why?" I couldn't see what Jay wanted me to see: there was no way that old woman could do worse to us than the middle-aged, nervous guy rehearsing speeches for his ex-wife.

"You are such a taint; you got to *think*. What if she wants to enslave us? Get us back for something our ancestors we don't even know maybe might have done to them? This is exactly what I meant when I said you need help figuring shit out. You'll never survive if you don't work out the possibilities. What would you do if we ran into a bear right now?"

There was no reasoning with him when he got this way. We waited. The night grew deeper, and once it was just the two bright yellow eyes of a car's headlights coming at us through the black mist, we decided to snatch a few hours of sleep before starting off again in the morning.

"All we need is an underpass," Jay said.

But once we found one—Jay made a pillow of his black backpack and lay with his feet pointing down the incline of the concrete, and I crouched beside him, not quite ready to relax against the filthy ground—my stomach started to loudly protest the fact that I had eaten only two candy bars and a few weeds for the entire day, and then Jay's stomach joined mine, the chorus of grumbles echoing pitifully.

"We don't have any money," I said, watching a shiny black beetle scuttle among the pebbles. "How will we get food to eat if we don't have any money? We already ate all the stuff you grabbed from your house. What if we *starve* out here?" All of a sudden, I longed for the easy option; if only I could be transported straight back to my neighborhood in my bedroom behind the door that could lock everyone else out. Maybe then I'd revert to being myself, to feeling okay— because running away hadn't been the quick fix for which I'd hoped. Inside, I still felt shitty, and now I was starving, too. "Maybe it's time to head home?" The thought that we could make all this go away excited me. "We could turn around. No one would know we'd left."

"Going back is the dumbest idea I ever heard," Jay said. But his voice was small, and I could tell that he was a little bit scared, too.

"Come on. It would be easy. Toshi"—I winced—"he'll be okay. Maybe he'll forget about the whole thing. I mean, Tosh is understanding, right? We'll talk to him, or…"

Jay's shoulders started shaking then, and I feared that some malevolent insect had bitten him, coursed its poison into his veins—but he was crying. "What's wrong?" I said, trying to tramp down the panic evoked in me by Jay's tears. I'd never seen his façade crumble this way before. "What's the matter?"

He fought with his body and soon the spasms stopped, but for a second there, he had emitted the same sorts of noises as when he was imitating some dumb, emotional girl.

"Fuck," he said, "don't ever tell anyone about this." He gasped once, twice, the air shuddering through him. "But Toshi," he said. "It's Tosh. He's dead."

The slope of the underpass seemed to steepen, and I plopped backwards onto my bottom to keep from following the flow of concrete down to the earth. "He's not dead. We didn't do anything that bad to him. Remember? He's not dead." Our skimpy meals and thirst and lack of sleep must all be working together on Jay, making him act crazy. "We just need some food and some rest and stuff; then don't you think you'll feel better?"

"He *is* dead. He killed himself. After the thing we did. I should have told you before, but, I don't know, I didn't want to say it. You might have done something stupid."

"No way," I said. "No he didn't. Your imagination made this up. What are you talking about? You've been with me the whole time. Maybe this was a nightmare, one that you remember way too much."

"I didn't want to have to show you this"—Jay reached into the backpack—"because I knew that you would freak, but Toshi left this in my room. He wanted me to find it. And I did this morning, when I went back to get the supplies, when you were waiting in the woods."

Jay handed me a piece of paper, a letter. It was a note signed by Toshi. I didn't want to touch it; I read it as fast as possible. *I had to do this… you embarassed me… I would never be able to live this down.*

"He wouldn't go through with it, though," I said. My words were tumbling one on top of the other. "Maybe he only wanted to scare us." I brushed hard at my arm, but the bugs I'd felt crawling there were nonexistent. I thought about how Toshi had bludgeoned that dog caught in the bear trap, how he'd been so intent on putting her out of her misery. I thought about how I'd decided, in a moment of fear, that it would be easier to kill myself than let Jay know the truth about what had happened between me and Tosh that night in Stella's bedroom.

"I figured it had to be a joke, too," Jay said, "but right after I found the note in my room, I turned on the news to check, and they were saying stuff like *local boy commits suicide, possibility of foul play,* blah blah blah, all this stuff, and then they flashed a picture of Toshi from the last yearbook."

"No way," I said. "No fucking way." My whole body was fighting this information; my pores were tightening up against the intrusion of it. "That one where he's wearing the bowtie?"

Jay nodded as he reached over and took Toshi's note from my hand. The paper sliced the pulp of my fingertip and I squeezed it to make the blood well, to prove to myself that I was alive and this wasn't just a dream.

"At first I was only having fun." He closed his eyes, but kept talking. "When we ran out of New Veronia, I mean. It sort of made the whole thing more exciting, running away from Knees after what we did. It was like an ending in a movie, I guess. I was maybe going to hide out with you for a day or whatever in the woods, mountain man up, and then go back. It's fun camping. Shooting squirrels. Getting away from the parents. I never thought we would *really* have to run."

"No way. No, no, no." All of a sudden, I could see myself from above, as if my eyeballs were hanging from the rebar that bristled the bottom of the underpass. My body looked sad down there, insignificant, with hairy ankles and a t-shirt stain shaped like a banana. I chewed the inside of my cheek and, rather than feel the rubbery skin between my teeth, my dangling eyeballs saw the contour of my cheek cave. Being removed like this, muted, let me bear it.

But then Jay snapped my body back together when he uncovered his eyes and looked at me. "Don't you get it? Toshi killed himself, but it's like *we* killed him. It really is. We can't go back."

My stomach shrunk down to a point, a sort of needle jabbed into my core. I doubled over, nursing it. "Please tell me this isn't true. It can't be true, because if it is, then nothing will ever be the same for us."

Tears were silently coursing down Jay's cheeks, a bizarre transformation of his face which made me understand that he was serious. This realization paralyzed me, and I traveled deep inside myself, searching through the crannies of my mind to see if there was a way I could will myself back, to travel back to before any of this had ever happened.

———

I couldn't tell how long it was before Jay sat up and poked me. "We're basically on the run from the law now," he said. "I mean, maybe not, depending on if Knees talked to anyone or whatever. Before he…. But the news did say 'foul play.' Maybe he left someone else a note, too. Maybe they're after us. And so what would one more tiny crime be?"

"What are you talking about?" I sat up straight—my whole body felt achy, as if I'd hiked a hundred miles—and brushed away some bits of grit stuck to my face.

"I'm talking about supper."

I nodded, relieved that we were moving past the topic of Toshi. If we were going to make it—it was cruel, but—if we wanted to survive, we needed to block him out, to forget as well as we could. We were alive, and in order to stay that way, we couldn't dwell in the world of death. One more mention of Toshi might break me down completely, and I was *done* crying in front of Jay, so I took the memory of that last night in New Veronia and rolled it up tight, then tucked it down into the folds of my brain.

"I *got* to eat," Jay said.

The underpass smelled like metal and wax and puke. Because my hunger prevailed despite this stench, I knew that I needed food, too, and soon. I could feel my bones growing inside of my skin, stretching out my organs, pulling my stomach thinner. Growing pains, my dad used to say when I'd rub my shins and complain. I asked Jay, "Are you saying we just steal? From where?" Taking Tony's mattresses, which had already been thrown out, was one thing; stealing from a store was another. Back in the fifth grade, a cashier had caught me lifting Necco wafers, and the horror instilled in me by the cashier's anger, the mayonnaise-smelling room they'd locked me in before the policeman came, the policeman's huge teeth, and the spanking my father inflicted on me made me wary of trying the experiment again.

Jay popped into a crouch and swiveled his head from side to side. "I see supper at…that gas station over there."

The Mobil's sign glowed at us from maybe a quarter mile off. "It's late," I said. "Don't you think they'll notice a couple of kids sneaking around in there?"

"We snatch some shit, then we take off. Totally out of this place. That's the beautiful thing about being on the move: you don't stick around long enough for people to *notice* you."

Jay had already made up his mind about what we were going to do. Maybe I was feeling kind of down about Toshi; and running away without saying goodbye to my dad, even though he'd been basically awful lately, not like a dad at all; and scared that we were getting closer and closer to my mom, who had made it pretty clear my whole life that she wanted nothing to do with me, and how would she take it when I showed up at her house in Florida with a ravenous disrespectful Jay in tow when I was supposed to still be in Delaware; and also my stomach was eating itself, making me miserable from the inside out. All these bad feelings resigned me to tailing along behind Jay as he walked into the Mobil store.

We beelined for the back, where a shoulder-high shelf of chips and candies mostly hid us from the cashier. Jay grabbed beef jerky, beer nuts, and licorice and stuffed the snacks down his pants; as soon as I saw him at it, I did the same, my mouth prickling with saliva at the thought of eating.

It must have been only about thirty seconds before we started back towards the front door. We had to walk right past the cashier to get out, and as we rounded the final aisle, my guts started to quiver in fear, which felt extra strange paired with the hunger already gnawing me. The man was staring at us, fingering the little plastic nametag pinned to the front of his yellow smock. Ten steps from the door, I had this lightened feeling; I knew that we would make it.

"Empty the drawer." Jay had stopped short directly in front of me. He pulled something out from under his shirt and pointed it at the man; the thing was metal; it looked like a gun. Curious, I watched the scenario.

"Empty it. *Now.* Give the money to him." Jay jerked his head in my direction.

In just a few seconds, my whole body had switched from feeling every current of the air conditioner, every crack between the floor tiles, to feeling nothing at all. The cashier had opened the drawer; he was piling bills on the countertop. His face had turned bright red and his eyes were bulging, but he was careful not to look at us. I couldn't think of a single thing to do besides reach out and scoop up the cash. It wasn't stacks of twenties like in the movies, but it was something. All of a sudden I realized that we were in charge here. In a mean little thrill of power, I snatched a Cadbury egg, the expensive kind they put by the checkout for impulse buyers.

We ran. We ran as fast as we could, not in the direction of our underpass, but towards another gas station on down the road.

"It's too bright over here!" I said. "They'll find us for sure. What the *hell* was that? Where'd you get a *gun*?"

"Muzzle up, Bennet; it's part of the plan." Jay, still holding the gun, pumped his arms as he ran, and for one gruesome moment I pictured the trigger going off beneath his chin, exploding his face into bloody pieces.

I said, "You didn't tell me about that last 'plan'! What the fuck, Jay? That was crazy. Be careful with that thing." I could barely keep up with him.

The road continued over a drainage ditch and towards a circle of parking lot lights that surrounded another gas station.

Jay said, "Fuck that. I know what to do." As we neared the parking lot lights, Jay slowed to a walk, casual-like, and zipped the gun into his backpack.

I stared at this crazy person, the moonlight glossing over his goatee so that his face looked more like a kid's, and I had to forcefully remind myself that he was my best friend, that I would follow him wherever. "How long have you been planning that?" I asked. "Did you get it off of some cop show or something?"

Jay strolled right over to a pickup hitched to a flatbed trailer and slipped beneath the trailer's tarp. I looked around, mouth agape, to see if anyone had noticed. It was quiet. I dove under the tarp with him and pulled the plastic shut behind us.

"What just happened?" I whispered. "What did you do? Hiding under here is part of the plan?"

Jay rolled onto his back and pulled his hands up behind his head. "That gas station sucked. Wish it had been a Wawa. Then we could have grabbed some real food." He pulled the beef jerky out of his pants and started to eat.

I lay stomach-down on splintery boards, and my feet seemed tangled up with some other junk back where I couldn't see. "We would have gotten away with just the food," I said. "What did we need all that money for?" But now that we had the cash, I couldn't deny that I was glad. I touched the wad of it in my pocket. This money would give us a little bit of security, at least.

"If you have money, you have everything," Jay said. "They been stealing money from us for years, and it's only right we take a little back."

"Who's been stealing from us?" I asked, but I shouldn't have, because next I had to listen to Jay's familiar rant about how our neighborhoods were being broken up, how we deserved payback, how we needed to demand respect.

As I half-listened to Jay, I fingered the bills, feeling transformed, rich and full of mystery. It was a powerful feeling, to think that I was cool.

"Somehow I knew this ride would be waiting for us." Jay patted the trailer. "We're special that way. Hey, give me the cash."

"Do you hear that?" I said as I handed over the money. I felt a little sorry to give it up, because it was a concrete reward for the fifty seconds of numbing fear I'd endured when Jay had pulled out his gun. "Sirens?" But before I could confirm the sound, the truck rumbled to life and the trailer started to move beneath us. "Where are we going?"

"That was easy." Jay snorted. "Man, that was so easy. If I'd known how easy…"

I unwrapped the expensive chocolate egg and shoved the

whole thing into my mouth. At first, it tasted delicious, but after a trickle of it had slid down my throat, all it made me feel was thirsty. "Jay, why'd you bring a gun?"

"We're on our own now." He crunched a handful of chips. "A bear could come, or we might need to hunt our food. A gun is just, like, a smart tool to have."

"But it doesn't have bullets, right?"

"Only a pussy carries around an unloaded gun. Man, without me, you would never survive."

After a half hour, the rattling of the trailer anesthetized my skin, and my head ached from my brain knocking around in there. I tried to sleep, but instead fell into a trance, the kind where all you're doing is waiting, and the waiting takes forever. I either dreamed or imagined that I was in limbo with Toshi, my dead friend Tosh, and the place had the most uncomfortable metal chairs.

My trance was finally broken when the truck slowed, probably taking an exit. "This is perfect," Jay said. "We've been driving long enough that we've got to be in another state. And crimes don't follow across state lines!"

"Quiet," I said. "I think he's almost stopped."

"So when he goes in to pay for his gas, we slip out and run for it."

"Where?"

"Back to the highway to catch another ride."

"But where are we, even? We don't know what way we have to go!" My breath was coming in gasps, and I worried all that rattling had shaken apart my nasal passages. Maybe I would never breathe right again. I had trusted Jay, trusted that he had a real plan. "Seriously, we could be *any*where."

"Shut up, Bennet, don't act like a girl."

The movement of the truck had stopped, even though my body still felt like it was going forward.

"Here's our chance. Here we go…" Jay lifted the tarp; everything outside was black.

In a panic, I realized that my legs had fallen asleep. "I can't run!" I said. "I can't run!" My throat ached from yelling quietly. "Don't leave me, Jay; my legs don't work!"

But Jay had already scrambled from beneath the tarp. I wiggled my toes furiously to get some feeling back down there, and then I staggered after him. I practically ran right into his back, because he stood motionless, staring at the man who must have been our driver for all those miles. We were parked in front of a clapboard house that glowed ghostly white in the night.

The man let his hand drop from where it was pressed against his heart, and then he slowly shook his head. "Now boys, don't you worry. I'm not mad. Used to be I did the same thing at your age. Why don't you come in and have some soup?"

The downstairs of the house lit up, and the windows cast an inviting glow out over the lawn.

"Nothing funny?" Jay said.

"Nothing funny." The man turned and made his way towards the house, and after a couple of seconds, we followed. Pins and needles shot up and down the muscles of my legs.

After we had both used the bathroom, we followed the smell of cheddar into the kitchen, where a black woman was ladling up three bowls of soup.

Decorative plates etched with roosters were propped atop the cupboards, and the counters were crowded with cookie cutters, copper pots, and a massive spice rack. You could barely see the fridge for all the kids' drawings that were plastered to it.

"I remember one time I planned to hitch to New York City," the man said as he took a seat at a small, round table in a corner of the kitchen. He gestured at the other chairs and we sat; Jay tucked the backpack securely between his feet. "I had this idea that it was nice up there. But the thing is? Here was as far as I got."

"Seems like you're doing well for yourself," Jay said. "You got a maid and all." He bobbed his chin at the woman arranging little crackers around the edges of the soups. The back of her dress pulled tighter, as if she'd felt Jay's nod and it had tensed her.

The man's face flushed a deep red. "No maid," he said. "That's my wife."

Jay laughed. I willed him to apologize, but so far as I knew, he never had, not once in his whole life. "Oh shit," Jay said after a minute, "you're serious? And so, what, you have little mulatto babies somewhere around here?"

"Hey, now," the man said, "you're in *my* house."

If Jay went for the gun, he'd have to unzip the backpack first; I'd have time to stop him.

"I thought you kids today were supposed to be progressive," the man said. His wife kept her back to us; her hands clenched the edge of the countertop. "Not small-minded bastards."

Jay knocked his chair to the ground with the force of his standing up. "We're out of here. I wouldn't eat that slop anyhow."

I grabbed the backpack that had become entangled with the chair legs and followed Jay towards the door. On the way there, he pushed over a vase, and a moment after it crashed, a kid started wailing piteously from somewhere on the second floor.

Beside the road, we broke through the underbrush and went a quarter mile back among the trees.

"Give me that backpack," Jay said. "What are you doing with this? You don't touch it. Only I touch it."

"I didn't want to leave it behind," I said as I handed it over.

Jay stopped at a part of the woods that looked like all the

other parts. "We'll bed down here for the night. Make a little shelter. It will kind of be like New Veronia."

The comparison made my stomach clench: New Veronia was what had gotten us into this mess. "What if they come looking for us? We're a little close, don't you think?"

"They won't do that," Jay said. "They're ashamed of themselves, is what they are, and they know I'm right. That flower pot I broke was a cheap piece of shit, anyhow. How many kids you think they have? Mixed up, is what those kids'll be. You and me, we have that advantage, at least."

But right then, I felt like every advantage had fled me, and a fierce jealousy for the children in their beds in that cozy house raged in my chest. "I wanted real food," I said. "The soup…"

"We got plenty of money. I'll buy you soup at the next place we find." He put me to work clearing stones, and all the while he was gathering branches, he murmured about why we had it better, why we would survive.

Without Jay talking sense to me, I would have fallen apart —though it was what Jay had done in the first place making me feel like I couldn't hold it together. Each day with him seemed to compound the craziness of our lives. But I was only making it worse thinking this way; instead, I needed to follow some advice from the bible, a quote that really struck me as the best way to get by: "Do not worry about tomorrow, for tomorrow will worry about itself. Each day has enough trouble of its own." So I guess a lot of people have felt this same way.

Once we'd made a little place to bed down for the night, I said, "Jay, how much money do we have, anyhow?"

He stuck his hand in the pocket with the money; he was calm and collected, just as if he hadn't pulled off his first armed robbery a few hours before. "Let me count." He sorted through the bills twice, holding them close to his eyes, tilting them towards the moonlight. "Two hundred and fifty-eight bucks."

"Huh." This amount seemed pretty huge, and for a minute, I thought that maybe we did have it better than those stupid kids in their warm beds with their mother to cook them breakfast: we were rich. But then I shifted against the hard ground and something sharp poked my back.

"Doesn't it feel weird?" I said. "Spending the night somewhere, but we have no idea where it is. What state it is, even."

"Not that weird. Think about it, Bennet: how many places have you been that you've *really* felt at home in? Or that you've *really* understood?"

Sometimes Jay surprised me with his serious ideas. Maybe they were always floating around in there, ready to make a point, but he only let them out when I needed to hear them most.

Chapter 16

I couldn't sleep. Dry leaves worked their way up the sleeves of my shirt and bugs—either real or imagined—tickled the back of my neck. Jay, who had passed out immediately, kept inching his butt up against mine, and so I kept scooching away. The Zimzee loved to find more than one boy together, and he could sense badness: if the monster was real, then Jay and I were the perfect targets. I tried to force my thoughts elsewhere—what if thinking of the Zimzee so much gave him power, embodied him, somehow—but I couldn't help myself. The dark reverted me back to being a scared little kid.

I must have started to feel like a real criminal for the first time that night. The Zimzee would be able to see straight through me to the things I had done to Toshi atop that stolen mattress in New Veronia (and the thing Toshi had done to himself later, the thing I couldn't at that moment think to myself), and it would know that I'd fled rather than face consequences, and then held up a mini-mart, stolen money, nurturing my criminal inclinations.

I pulled Stella's panties out of my pocket and, for the first time, huffing them didn't make me horny. Instead, I thought about how they belonged to her, and about how much I wanted to talk to her right then, and maybe because it had been such a trying day or maybe because my head felt light and fuzzy and not quite a part of me, I made a sort of sock puppet out of her panties, a panty puppet, and then the puppet asked me how I was doing and it apologized for being so mean to me that day in the cafeteria, but that was what happened in school, it made you mean, and then it smoothed the hair back from my forehead, which encouraged me to open up, to tell Stella that I was more scared than I'd ever been, that maybe her brother was totally unhinged, but even if he was, I felt compelled to go along with him. I would probably do anything for him, bite off my own thumb, shoot a cashier in the teeth, renounce my love for Stella, even though she was my beautiful shining star. I told her how Jay was the only one who cared about me, probably he'd been the only one to *ever* care about me, and that meant a lot, it basically meant I owed Jay my life, and so even if he had some meanness at his core, I was bound to him forever. Jay was all I had left.

The night went on and on until the first strips of sunlight crept their way up from the bottom of the sky, and that lightness made me think we would be safe.

My tongue felt dry as a wafer, but the backpack with its half-full water bottle was tucked beneath Jay's head, so I licked at the gritty droplets of dew that the leaves had collected in the dark.

Somehow Jay got a decent rest during our four hours atop that pile of sticks, because he woke up ready to figure out where we were and from there, how to get on down to Florida.

"All we need is a road sign," he said, wandering back in the direction we'd come from last night.

"We should have brought a map."

"You think my parents just have some old map of Florida

lying around? Or did you think I had time to go to the map store in the middle of our running away?"

"Sorry," I said. "I was just thinking."

The air felt crisp, on the verge of fall, though in Delaware the tail end of summer was obvious on the edge of every morning. To be in a place with a name I didn't know made the world seem meaner, more threatening. Huge insects fell onto my skin from the treetops—but these were just dead leaves. Men yelled at us—but it was only a deep-throated, unfamiliar birdcall. Movement caught the corner of my eye, and I stepped closer to Jay, uncertain about the types of predators found here. Wherever *here* was.

Finding myself so dislocated reminded me of my first day of school in Delaware. My dad had driven me there because he needed to sign some papers at the front desk, and the route had consisted of so many turns onto roads that appeared identical to one another that I wondered if, some-how, we were actually staying in place. And then, when we finally did make it to the school, the strangeness continued. I remember that the secretary working the front desk had a jar of bacon and a Styrofoam cup of coffee right next to her pencil holder, and the similar way that the bacon and pencils poked skyward seemed obscene. She welcomed my father to town, patted her frizzy bangs, and told him the Amish made the best chocolate bacon and you could buy it cheap at the sale. I knew then that we'd landed in a place as foreign as Russia. But after a while, I got used to it, and now here I found myself, all these miles off, missing it.

Jay led us straight back to the road. The stripes between the opposite lanes were a different shade of yellow than in Delaware, another detail that made home feel far, far away.

"Road sign," Jay was mumbling, "road sign, road sign." Something green on a pole shimmered up ahead, and we kept moving toward it. When we got there, it said Berea Wash.

"Shit." Jay shook his head. "Not helpful. But we'll figure it out soon: we just find a road with north one way and south the other, and take the south way."

"How do you know we're supposed to go south?"

Jay knocked a knuckle against his head. "There's no more south than Florida."

"Well—maybe we're already *in* Florida."

"Quit dreaming," Jay said.

We walked along the road for a while, and not many cars passed, but each one that did, Jay stuck out his thumb. I tried to catch a glimpse of the license plates, but the cloud of dust that followed the vehicles made it impossible for me to check the plates' state. I was nervous that the folks Jay had insulted the night before would find us. Sometimes he did the stupidest things for basically no reason, acting brutish even when people were being kind, but there wasn't any stopping his fits. They were like gobs of bile come up from the dark place inside him, and if he didn't spit them out, he would poison himself. Or it could be that the bile was a sign he was poisoned already.

The small road we were walking along merged into a slightly less small road, and we passed a man mending a fence at the edge of a field. Jay hailed him. "We would be much obliged if you would tell us where we are, exactly, and maybe point us towards the biggest intersection around."

Jay had never said "much obliged" in his life, and even through my distress, it struck me how adaptable he was, telling the people what they wanted to hear in order to get his way.

The man paused in his work. "Boys, this is Summers County."

"In the state of…?"

The man shook his head. "West Virginia."

I chewed on my cheek: we had gone the wrong way. Maybe we weren't meant to make it to Florida. Maybe we were meant to go right back where we'd come from and face whatever punishment was waiting at home. I turned so that Jay wouldn't notice the anguish on my face. West Virginia was a sign: fate was taking us back; we shouldn't have run away.

———

Jay and I started to walk the way the man had pointed, the direction we'd been headed already.

"Did you see that guy's overalls?" Jay said. "How do you even get that many holes in overalls? They must be ancient."

"Jay?" I said. "Jay? I've been thinking." I hurried up alongside him.

"Must be because he works so hard, but he's still poor."

"Maybe we ought to go back," I said.

"I have all these ideas, so many good ideas about helping us get our jobs back. It's not fair how all our money flows out to people who ain't even real Americans. It's bullshit."

"Maybe this is a sign, since we got closer to home, and not further away."

"Most of them don't even pay taxes, it's true, and we're forced to pay the taxes, and so we carry them. Did you know that my dad lost his job a few days ago? He just got into a little tiff with this guy on the floor, not even worth it to call the guy his coworker, just a little tiff and those bammers toss him."

"That's awful," I said. "Maybe he needs you, back in Delaware…"

"It's so tough. Not providing for the family makes him angry, more angry than usual, and there's so much shit in the world to be angry about. I figured out something because of it: all a man wants to do is work. He wants to make good for his family and his country. But if those others are stealing from him, then what's the point?"

"Jay, *listen*. Maybe we ought to go back. To Delaware, I mean."

Finally, Jay looked at me. He stopped his relentless forward walk and grabbed my shoulder. "I thought we got over this. You want to give up? When we're just getting started? You want to give up now, at the easy part?"

"It's not giving up," I said. "It's just going back. I mean, really, we weren't there; we had nothing to do with the incident." Internally, I cringed at my use of this word. "And then once this whole episode is over, things will probably be fine, and we can do normal stuff, I don't know, find some girls for New Veronia..." The thought made me sick, but I figured it might get Jay to agree with me.

"And then," Jay said, "once we start going back, you'll just want to turn around again. I think what you really want is to be nowhere. You're scared to go to Florida, but you'd be scared to go to Delaware, too, so just nut up and get on with it."

"I'm not scared," I said. "But we don't even know where we are..."

"You want to go back," Jay said, contemplative. "You want to go back to an empty house. Your dad probably left on his road trip and you don't have a house. You want to go back to get sent to Florida anyway because your dad don't want you. Or maybe you want to go back so you'll get thrown in juvie. Or *jail*, even, depending on what Knees said to people without us there to defend ourselves. Any of this sound smart to you?"

I bit my lip; against my tongue, it felt like a worm. Jay was the smarter of us, even though I always did better in school. I was so stupid; my old life wasn't at home waiting for me, because things had already started to change even before I'd fled. It wasn't like I could return to school alongside the impossible ghost-presence of Toshi. My dad didn't have a job; we didn't have money; he didn't want this wicked teenaged thing I'd grown up into. I'd have to move to Florida anyway. Running off probably hadn't been a punishment to my father at all: I bet that he'd celebrated my sudden absence. Jay had known long before me that the only way for us right now was forward and away.

I didn't say anything. I just started walking towards the road south.

———

The forward motion of walking, the physical expense of it, helped me to remember that everything changed all of the time. I would never be able to get back to where I'd been before New Veronia, so there was no point in trying. From now on, I would listen to Jay; at least he had a vision of our future.

We came upon a gas station with a mini-mart attached, and in a flash, I relived our holdup of the Mobil. Sweat broke out across my brow. Jay strode toward the front door and I hesitated for only a second before I remembered the promise I'd just made to myself about Jay and his vision and our future.

By the time I got inside, Jay was working the condiment dispensers over a foot-long hotdog, so I followed his lead. My stomach contracted and expanded like an abused balloon; I couldn't wait to be a glutton. We each loaded two hotdogs with condiments and started eating even before we got to the cash register. I figured that a hotdog was only a buck, and we had a couple hundred, so probably Jay would just pay for us like a normal person. Up at the counter, Jay gave the cashier money stolen from the other mini-mart, and then he asked her for a piece of cardboard. After she handed it over along with his change, he used the pen attached to the counter by a chain, the one that people signed their checks with, to scribble FLORIDA on the cardboard.

Then Jay headed outside while I ran to the toilet.

There in the bathroom, holding my dick in one hand and my second hotdog in the other made me laugh—it was the first time I'd forgotten all the reasons I shouldn't laugh since we'd left Delaware. For a moment the release felt good, and then guilt overtook me, and I ignored my inclination to wonder about why.

When I came out, I didn't see Jay anywhere around; he'd ditched me. It was like that time our class had taken a trip to Busch Gardens, and I'd had to beg my dad for the entrance fee, and I'd looked forward to the trip for months and months, to me and Jay (Toshi hadn't been able to afford to go) screaming as the roller coaster loop-de-looped, but as soon as we got past the ticket booth, Jay disappeared. I spent the whole class trip miserably wandering around, looking for him; I didn't go on a single ride. If Jay had left me this time, I wouldn't repeat that abused dog routine; I wouldn't sniff around, hoping to find him. I would have to get my own self down to Florida.

But then Jay rounded the corner of the store, and my whole body surged with relief: I wasn't alone. He hadn't left me. Jay kept walking as if nothing at all had happened—that was the amazing thing, that in his mind, nothing had.

"What were you doing?" I asked.

"Guy back there with a radio." Jay pointed with his hotdog. "I was trying to find a station." He held up the cardboard FLORIDA. "Check it out: this is our ticket." With a huge bite of hotdog in my mouth, I was unable to reply, so he went on. "The drivers see this and they know exactly what we want. If they're heading there, or that way, they'll pick us up."

I swallowed. "Maybe we should try to clean up a little. So that we look like good kids. Right? Or like we won't get the upholstery dirty." Every crevice on my body felt grimy, and my hair was styled by its own grease.

Jay looked me up and down. "You're fine. How about me?" He rubbed hard at the back of his neck as if polishing his tattoo.

"You look okay." His blond crew cut had grown out just enough to catch a few twigs and pieces of leaves. I would have brushed them out if I'd been just a little bit taller. He had a dark smudge on one cheek and a red scratch on the other, and his clothes were streaked with grime. "But do we smell?"

"I don't smell anything but this hotdog," Jay said as he took the last bite. Yellow mustard smeared the corner of his mouth.

"I guess we're all right." I shrugged. Maybe we would snag a ride out of pity.

At the intersection, we sat down in the shade. When the traffic picked up a little, Jay ambled over to the road headed south and held the sign just below his chin. After a couple hours, when I was dozing in a patch of grass, Jay shouted my name, and I felt my whole body pop upright before I'd even opened my eyes, before I was conscious, really. That felt pretty strange, like I was a puppet and Jay held the strings.

The dynamic between Jay and me had changed. We'd always been a crew; it had always been me, Jay, and Toshi, and even when Toshi wasn't around, there was still his *presence*, the *idea* of him. But now that he'd never be a part of our group again, that presence was lost, and me and Jay were just a pair. Without Toshi, we were lopsided, maimed. But already we were healing up, relearning who did what, and becoming much closer in the process, almost like family, like brothers. Sometimes it bothered me that Jay still hadn't told me the story of his missing brother, but then again, I hadn't asked. I needed to, though—if we were going to become tight as real brothers, I had to know everything I could about whoever might have held that role before me.

Chapter 17

Jay's plan worked out great: his cardboard got us into Florida the very next afternoon. That big, juicy orange for the O—I saw the state's welcome sign for myself, or I wouldn't have believed that we were there.

"It's Florida," I whispered to Jay so that the driver wouldn't hear the awe in my voice. I was closer to my mother than I'd been in over a decade. I hadn't really thought that we would make it, that we would find her, but seeing that welcome sign made me believe it was possible.

"Told you," he said. "I told you we'd get to Florida. See?

No problem." Jay kept fiddling with the radio. He switched from one brand of static to another until the driver told him to shut it off.

"You got relatives here, I hope," the driver said into the ensuing silence. "Someone to take care of you, I hope."

"We do," Jay said. "Going to see my older brother."

I shot my eyes over to him, but he was staring at his lap.

"You get straight to him, then. Don't want to get caught up in anything. Lots of all kinds, see? All kinds you'll find around a swamp."

The guy dropped us off before he turned toward his house. On either side of the road, which looked like the sort nobody ever used, vegetation grew huge and looming, a hundred shades of green closing in.

"It's not that different from Delaware here," Jay said.

"But there are alligators, right?"

"Crocodiles. Wouldn't it be wild to see a bear and a croc fight?"

I barely heard him, so preoccupied was I with the question I'd been holding just behind my lips. "Is there something you haven't told me?" His eyes quivered, sort of like a scared animal's, a look I hadn't seen on him before, so I figured that I could press him. "Like about some brother?"

"Oh," Jay said, "you want to know about that?" He almost sounded relieved, and I told myself that of course he'd been meaning to divulge all his secrets, of course he told me everything. He'd just forgotten about this one.

"It was a long time ago," he said. "Before you moved here."

I nodded: this all fit. We were walking slowly down the road, heading south because that felt better than being still.

"It was like my second trip. My second or third trip hunting with my dad and my older brother. I was seven, but he was even older than Stella, thirteen, I guess. My dad could sit for hours in the hunting blind, but I was a stupid kid and I got restless, bothering my dad, so my brother took me looking for rabbits or whatever around the pond. We walked out there, and when we were walking back, we decided to play a game. Sneak up on my dad in the blind. He always said he could hear us from a mile off, and we wanted to prove him wrong. Only, a hundred yards out, I stopped being careful. I rustled a bush, and my brother got shot.

"Even when he dropped, he was quiet. I thought maybe we were still playing the game. Still trying to sneak up on the blind. I didn't say anything for a while; I just kind of watched him while he bled out. Maybe I was in shock. If I had known back then all the stuff I know now, like how to tourniquet or pack a wound and all this other survivalist stuff, maybe he wouldn't have died, but I guess he did. We put him in the back of the truck like we would have any deer. Sometimes you got to be practical, I mean, we couldn't have him up in the cab of the truck with us. Wouldn't have been practical."

Jay relayed all this in a stoic, unvarying tone. He stared straight ahead at the road we were walking. It was like his brother hadn't been a secret at all, hadn't been difficult for him to talk about, and he'd just needed a reminder that he hadn't told me yet.

"Your dad shot him?" I said.

"No! No way."

"Then who did?"

"Dad swore he hadn't fired in that direction at all, so it must have come from somewhere else, I don't know. It was hunting season."

Our road started to grow narrower, and the sky ticked towards darkness.

"When my dad was real mad, he used to say, 'I could kill you off. Wouldn't bother me none. Your mom and me could make a replacement in nine months.' "

"That's awful," I said.

"No, you don't get it: he was trying to make me feel

better. To show me I didn't take much away from him when I made all that noise and got my brother shot."

"Oh." As the air counted down towards night, it became heavy and wet, not like it was going to rain, but like each thread of dark wove into a web for catching dew.

"But," Jay said, thoughtful, "I hadn't seen any other hunters out that day."

"Why'd you tell that guy we were going to see your brother?"

"I don't know. It sounded more killer than saying we were going to find your mommy."

"Do you think about him a lot?"

"Not really at all." As he walked, Jay kicked a stone ahead of us, always landing it directly in front of him, precise as if it were a soccer ball. "One thing I always thought was off: black people, they don't hunt. They'd rather get food stamps than go out and shoot their own food. It's strange, is what it is. Don't make sense."

I had to admit that Jay saying stuff like this did make him sound like a skinhead, but I couldn't call him out, not after the way he'd just opened up to me. As we walked, I thought about the story of Jay's brother, but I couldn't figure out why it scared me. It had all happened so long ago, before I'd even heard of Delaware. When I felt sure that Jay had told me everything, that he wouldn't say anymore, I filed away Jay's history and turned towards the practical. "Now where do we go?"

Jay shrugged. "It's your mom. Figure out where she lives."

Something rustled a lime green bush beside me; panic rose in my throat. The road was cracked like an elephant's skin and barely wide enough for two cars; we should have gotten out near to the freeway, like our driver had offered, but we'd decided instead to go as far south as he could take us.

Jay groaned. "How did we get all the way here without ever getting a map?" He sat on the side of the deserted road, his butt right next to the creeping green and brown and yellow stuff that grew wildly all around us. He covered his face with his hands. This wasn't how a leader was supposed to act.

"Jay," I said, crouching close to him, "what's wrong?" Maybe telling me about his brother had taken more out of him than I'd realized. "We'll figure it out. Look how far we got already. We'll find my mom. We'll be totally fine. Look, sometimes I feel like"—I built myself up; I was going to say it —"we're brothers. You and me. Right?"

Instead of say that yeah, that was right, Jay's body slumped like a noodle, and my fingertips pricked with grief. I rubbed them hard against my closed eyes.

Just on the cusp of full dark, I got Jay to follow me away from the road, a few yards into the swamp, where we sat on a log that caved in gently beneath us. White bugs swarmed the ground, but they were only termites; they wouldn't hurt us.

"I thought that they would find me by now," he said.

"What are you talking about?"

"The Eye Whites." His voice sounded weak and out of character; maybe he was delirious. "You would think that someone, one of them, at least, would have seen my tattoo."

"What do you mean—what about your tattoo?"

"You know, the Eye Whites thing." He touched the tattoo at the back of his neck. "It's a mark sort of like so we can recognize each other. It's political. At the conference, everyone had it. It's on chicks' ankles. Or guys' biceps. Or wherever. We should get you one."

"Maybe." But I'd always thought that, if I got a tattoo, it would be words, a quote, some clever Shakespeare quote that people would think was funny and smart. "You never told me your tattoo was part of this whole political thing that you're into. You said it was a zebra eyeball, once."

He blew air through his lips. "Sometimes I like to make shit up. To mess with you." For some reason, this made me feel like Jay had been keeping a fat, monster secret, even though I knew he wouldn't see it that way. If the Eye Whites were a permanent part of his body, then he had to feel pretty obsessed with them.

"The thing is, I thought they would find us before we got all the way to here. They're great; they would take us in... there's this network. We stick together; we got to. But I guess we're lost."

"You wanted us to go stay with the Eye Whites? Instead of my mom? Why didn't you tell me before?" The termites glowed a little in the dark, and I followed their paths with my eyes.

"You acted all prickly, calling us 'skinheads' and all that, like we're some creepy gang, so I figured you had to nut up first. Then you'd be surprised when you met them; you'd be so happy. You know what?" His voice grew stronger. "There are white people we're against, too. Those Greenies. They want to save a tree, a tree's more important than a job. They want the factories to disappear to get rid of their smoke-stacks. We'd stomp those bammers. We're against them, too. We have principles."

"But maybe it's better this way," I said. "My mom will cook for us, remember? She'll have a room for us." Jay's Eye Whites sounded less appealing than my mom, but Jay and I were in this together, and we *were* brothers—even if what he said was inane, we relied on each other like brothers. They were just words.

"You'll figure it out for yourself." He flicked a termite off the back of his hand. "I mean, all you got to do is look around at the world, is live a little. You know why we're called the Eye Whites? Because that's the part of someone you see, when they get scared: the whites of their eyes. And our enemies, those people against us, they're always scared, and that's because they know they're wrong."

"But they aren't here. They didn't find you."

"Yeah," he said. "I know." He curled up tighter into himself as the termites made a path over his left shoe. "It's my fault," he mumbled. "I couldn't find their radio station. They have one somewhere around here. Ham stuff. And I didn't see anyone in the truck stops, but maybe they had their tattoos covered..." Jay sat there, kind of catatonic, and so I gathered as many dry sticks and bits of leaves as I could find around the perimeter of our little camp, dug a pit, and used our book of matches to start a fire. The flames reached up, a couple dozen grabbing at the air, and just as quickly they died down, everything burned away before I could even unwrap my Slim Jim to warm it. Jay held his hands over the curled-up worms of dead leaves, the first move he'd made to interact with the world since he'd acknowledged that the skinheads weren't coming to save us.

We bedded down on the ground. Dampness seeped from the earth where my hip pressed against it. I had this feeling like, now that Toshi was gone, Jay and I were the last two people on earth. We'd been left here in the reeking dark after everyone else had escaped to somewhere better.

I had to shake this idea out of my head; I was starting to scare myself. "We'll find my mom," I said to Jay. "We'll find a phone book. It'll be easy. At her house, you can use the radio all you want."

Jay said, "What's she like? Your mom."

Closing my eyes didn't make much difference, it was that dark. But I closed my eyes anyway to try and say something that might make Jay feel better. "She's pretty," I said, "with blond hair; what do they call it? Ash blond. But she was real nice; she would bake you cookies whenever you asked. Every Sunday, she went to church. She liked those shows where you guessed the price of stuff, everyday stuff like toasters and end tables. Real nice lady." Some of this I truly remembered, but some I made up because I thought Jay would like it. "Probably as soon as we find her she'll bake us something. Casserole, brownies. Something." Maybe she would be happy to see me. Maybe it was a whole big misunderstanding that I figured she never cared about me, never thought of me. Maybe there was another explanation for her cutting off all contact with her son, like my dad had warned her away, or he'd acted like such a drunk that she couldn't stand to be around him. I guessed I'd be finding out pretty soon.

After Jay fell asleep, I tossed back and forth, my heart racing. No matter how deeply I tried to breathe, my blood kept whooshing anxiously through my veins. I reached into my pocket for Stella's panties, which I wrapped around my right hand into a puppet. My knuckles made little bumps for the eyes and, I don't know, it was stupid, but I felt comforted looking at this strange, sweet purple thing. "Stella," I whispered, "I feel a little crazy here. I mean, look at me—talking to you this way."

"It's perfectly understandable," Stella said.

"But if Jay saw me doing this, he would hate me."

Stella said, "No, he wouldn't feel that strongly about you: you're nothing to him. Jay doesn't care about you. Not really."

"Don't be mean," I said. "He does. Even if he doesn't show it. I need him."

"You don't *need* anybody."

I petted the purple face. Stella was brutal in the way of siblings, but somehow she knew: once things were normal, I'd never speak to Jay again. We wouldn't be friends. And this fact took the top off of my head.

But out here, where I felt lost and hungry and thirsty and, pitifully, scared like a little kid, I needed him. He was still my best friend. "Something will happen soon," I said; "maybe I'll make something happen, but not yet." This moment between us, this conversation, had framed out a whole new dimension of my world, which had been revolving tight around Jay for years. Before, I had felt certain that I'd never be able to change the pattern, but that was the night I started to think that I could.

I must have dozed, because I woke up feeling chilled. The night air was mostly warm, but something had frightened me into consciousness. Then I heard it again: a long, low howl that crescendoed into a high-pitched yelp. My arms prickled over with goosebumps as I unwrapped Stella's panties from my fingers and stuffed them back into my pocket.

"Jay." I shook his shoulder. "Jay, what was that?" He pushed me away, but I pinched him until he woke. "What kind of wild animals do they have out here?" I whispered.

He sat bolt upright. "Crocodiles," he said. "We should sleep in a tree. Bears can climb trees, but I know how to handle a bear."

"That's not what I heard. It was a wild dog, a wolf, maybe. Crocodiles don't yelp."

We listened for a while, but the sound didn't come again, so we climbed up a tree and kind of slid down into the big pocket the branches all made where they came off from the trunk. Up there, I thought about the Zimzee, his scratchy bark fingers slipping off his victims' skin, his dark mouth and blood-covered wood chipper teeth, his breath smelling like malt liquor.

"Every year," I said, "thirteen people under the age of eighteen are eaten by wild animals in Florida."

"What?" Jay said.

"One in eighteen people will get malaria. One in twenty-seven, rabies." At first, I didn't know why I was making up statistics, but then it dawned on me that I liked the way it pushed panic into Jay's breath. "Five in eighty-seven will contract giardia."

"Stop it," Jay said. "What's wrong with you?"

My channeling Toshi in this way, through his obsession with statistics, upset Jay, and this relieved me because it showed that Jay had cared for our friend, after all. "Four in five will drive drunk, but only sixteen percent of those will get caught."

"Stop it, man," Jay said, his voice breaking. He was thinking about Toshi; he was remembering how close we'd all been. I was glad for this proof that he wasn't too different from me.

Jay gasped. "I need you to stop."

I stopped. I couldn't think of any more statistics, anyhow; I was too tired.

I woke to Jay clutching my arm. "Bennet, I heard it! It could be anything. Some Florida thing." He was panting; I knew that he was thinking about the Zimzee, too. Maybe he'd been having a nightmare, because normally, he would hide his distress; I saw fear in him even more seldom than sadness. "What are we going to do?"

The noise did sound closer, and I thought that I could hear footsteps, a heavy thing moving towards us. I gripped the tangle of branches that held me.

"What if," Jay said, his voice deadly serious, "what if it's the devil?"

"Shut up. It might be able to hear us." I worried he was losing his marbles, that he might give us up on purpose because his guilt over Toshi was finally choking him. *The devil*, he'd said.

The noise came again; I felt certain I heard steps.

And then something huge, looming, broke through the foliage of our little clearing, and I begged my heart to explode right then so that I wouldn't have to feel myself being skinned. The thing had a tail, a thin, flapping triangle of flesh, and it walked on two legs over to our pitiful campfire and kicked at the ashes. For a second, I felt relief—it was a man, the dingy white of his t-shirt making him visible in the almost-dawn—and then his face turned towards us up in the tree and my stomach dropped straight through the earth's crust.

———

"What you boys doing up there?" The man's eyes and mouth were holes in the predawn, and his large body moved loosely, as if every joint were double-bending. A black strap bisected his chest, the sort of strap that held a shotgun, and his strange tail twitched from side to side.

"Was that you howling?" Jay asked.

"You sleeping up there? How about you come on down."

"I don't think we should go," I said quiet as I could to Jay. At the tree trunk's base nestled our black backpack. We were stupid to have left it so far away.

"You think that man can't climb a tree?" Jay said. "He can climb a tree."

"Get down. Now."

Jay and I didn't hesitate any longer; we each held onto a different branch and dropped ourselves to the ground. In the second I was hanging, I felt acutely aware that my bellybutton was showing, that it made a perfect gaping target for the man. I reached for the backpack, but the man told me no. "I'm a quick shot," he said.

Once we stood before him, a ways off from the tree and our pack, he brought his tail around to the front. It was an alligator, a small one, maybe two feet long, with a rope tied like a leash around its snout. "Dinner," he said, and the dangling thing twitched angrily. He dropped it and set a foot over the rope. "You're in my swamp. Tariff to pass. So, give me all your money." He held out a hand; his skin was tanned a dark, wrinkled brown, like bark. Like the Zimzee. But he was a white man, and even through my fear, I realized that was wrong: Jay's Zimzee, the one his father had scared him with, was black.

"Sure," I said, "that's okay. Jay, give it over. Just give it."

"We don't have any money," Jay said, but his hand burrowed deep into his pocket, where he kept the stolen cash; he fiddled his fingers around in there.

The Zimzee growled and then hawked a loogie onto the ground near Jay's feet. "Don't lie to me."

"Okay," I kept saying, hoping my voice sounded soothing to the Zimzee, "okay…"

The Zimzee casually reached behind his back for his sawed-off shotgun, then pointed it straight at Jay's head. "Money," he said. His eyes went on and on, omnipotent.

Finally Jay pulled the bills out from his pocket and defiantly tossed them at the Zimzee's feet.

The Zimzee shook his head like we were the dumbest pair he'd ever come across, and probably he was right. He jerked the barrel of his gun towards Jay and said, "Get down there and pick it up and hand it to me nice. Then you get out of my sight. How old is you two, anyways? Out on your own."

Jay slowly got to his knees and bent, his neck looking vulnerable and dirty, towards the cash.

"Fuck," the Zimzee said, staring down at Jay. He poked the barrel of his gun against the back of Jay's neck, right where the tattoo marked him.

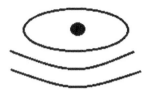

The ground was creeping up around my shoe, wetting my toes. In fact, my whole body felt wet, a trickle down my back, my underarms swampy, my groin like a Jacuzzi, like something bubbling in there.

"You piece of shit." The Zimzee's voice, a smoker's growl, grated against the insecty hum of the vegetation. Like proving me right, he pulled out a hand-rolled cigarette. When he lit it, the burning smell floated above the thick musty loam where I'd thought for a moment that Jay and I might be the last two people on earth. "You're one of them, huh? That means a tariff is too good for you. You owe more." Smoke inched out through his nostrils and for some reason it scared me, to see something solid burned into nothing before this man's lips.

"But you told us we could go," I said. "You have our money now. All of it." I pulled Jay upright so that he was standing beside me again. "That's everything."

"You're those Eye Whites," the Zimzee said, and the way he talked, it was like he was chomping the tobacco smoke.

"And proud of it." Jay tried to straighten himself, but his shoulders still curled inward.

A slow, cruel smile cleaved the Zimzee's face. "You know what you mean by that? You get what you're calling yourself?"

"I'm calling myself a real man."

"They took my boy," the Zimzee said. "Now he's one of their gang. I don't know him no more."

"So they're around here?" Jay asked, excited. "Where's their place?"

"Like I said." The Zimzee spat bits of tobacco onto the ground. "Plain tariff is too nice for an Eye Whites. Here's what I'll have you do."

During those long seconds before he came out with it, I must have aged a decade, because by the time he told us, I knew my adolescence was over.

"I'll let you get off," he said, "after the two of you grummet each other here. Give me a look."

The alligator, Dinner, whipped its body in an attempt at escape, but all it affected was a crackle like small-time fireworks against some dead leaves. This was the universe's way of getting me back, of bringing it all full circle. We'd met him only a few minutes ago, but I felt as if he'd had us imprisoned for weeks. "But we already paid you," I said. "We already—"

He interrupted: "That wasn't really no ask."

The Zimzee settled himself down on the same termite-occupied log we'd used as a bench the night before. He held his sawed-off shotgun in one hand as if it were a cheap can of beer, not paying too much attention to it, but not about to let it go, either. Dinner lay docile at his feet.

There once was a time when the slightest provocation— when the opposite of a provocation—would get me hard in an instant, but my cock hadn't stirred in days. Maybe being on the road, or not eating much, or the last time I'd had a boner… something like that must have robbed me of the quick-trigger teenage-given right to an erection.

"He wants to make a sort of live porn out of us," I whispered to Jay. "That's all." For some reason, the idea made me giddy. I could be fucked by Jay in the ass, almost like a reversal of what I'd done to Tosh, and then I would be free and I could go on my merry way and never have to look at Jay's sick sad hole of a face ever again. I could find my mom and see what she was like and then grow up on the other side of this godforsaken swamp.

"Hurry up, boys. Make something happen." The Zimzee's shotgun goggled at us through its barrels, two close-together, stupid looking eyes.

I put my hands up under Jay's shirt. His body felt softer than it should, with the sharp poke of bones close beneath the puffy skin. I closed my eyes and thought of a porn magazine I'd seen where the ropes were so tight across the women's breasts that it looked like their flesh was about to split.

Jay said, "I don't want to do this."

"Muzzle up, man. Come on." Never before had I been the stronger of us, but somebody had to keep it together, to get us out of this. I grabbed the front of his shorts. The fabric was grimy, and it felt like I was touching earth. "He could shoot us. I really think he would. We've got to." I thought about Stella; Stella and Jay were sort of the same person, genetically. But still I couldn't get hard.

Jay's eyes skittered back and forth, and I could see a wild flit behind his pupils, or maybe I just saw that he'd given up. But he nodded, and that was all the signal I needed to get to work.

"Your hip bones," I said to Jay as I pulled down his shorts. They rose sharply from the concave bowl of his stomach. "It's okay. Remember: just concentrate." Excitement was riling up my stomach. Not the sexy kind, but the kind that told me any minute now, I could be skipping away from this hell and back to civilization. I had to come, and then I would be free. Maybe I'd never come again. Maybe I'd stop using my cock altogether as a personal punishment for the reason we'd left Delaware.

Jay now stood naked before me, but he wasn't making any moves to take off my own clothes, so I did it for him. There we were, our socked feet against the loamy soil, vines hanging down from the tree above us, two Adams after the apples got chewed. My mother would probably take me to church with her on Sundays; maybe the priest would topple over if I confessed this sin.

"Here I go," I said, getting to my knees. I worked hard on Jay with my mouth, doing to him the things I'd imagined girls doing to me, being careful with my teeth, breathing through my nose as little as possible because of the onion tang of his unwashed skin, and when I got him to half-mast, I felt proud. One step closer, I thought. I wouldn't spend another second more than I had to with that swampy Zimzee. My jaw ached from the sucking.

"Hey," the Zimzee said, "now put it in his bootie." He'd unleashed his own inflamed cock from his pants and was stroking it languidly.

"We've got to get down on the ground," I said to Jay, and I didn't add, like animals.

But that was okay: we were animals fighting for our freedom. I lifted my hand to Jay's shoulder—I'd gotten taller, or maybe Jay was stooped over; I didn't have to hold my hand so high—and told him that everything would be okay, but he only shrugged me off.

"No," the Zimzee said. "You put it in the one with the tattoo. Fuck the Eye Whites out of him. This is something they would off you for, you know that, boys? They won't have you after you done this."

The tattoo, Jay's godawful tattoo had trapped us. If the Zimzee hadn't seen it, he would have taken our money and left, but Jay had to screw up everything for me once again. I switched places with Jay and fumbled with the soft head of my cock there at his asshole; Jay's muscles were tightening up against my intrusion.

"Come on." The Zimzee snarled. "You don't want me to come over there and show you how it's done." He shook his fat cock at us.

I spat into my hand and rubbed it over Jay's backside, and I tried and tried until finally I was fucking him.

"Don't disappoint me, now," the Zimzee said.

"We're almost done." I gasped. "Almost done."

The Zimzee stood; I saw his feet coming closer. I worried that he might kill us. But instead he shot yellow-tinged cum across the back of Jay's head. A hot dollop of it fell onto my arm. As he zipped up, he said, "Now you're going to follow me. I'm to make for certain you don't go the way of my boy. Come on. Get dressed."

I fumbled with my clothes; he *was* going to kidnap us, just like in the ghost stories.

Jay and I dressed as fast as we could, like maybe the scraps of cloth would protect us. "Dinner," Jay said, pointing.

The alligator, its rope trailing, had toddled into the swamp.

"Shit," the Zimzee said as he ran after it. The gun knocked against his side. With each of his steps, my blood pounded harder. My leg muscles twitched.

When a tree half-obscured the Zimzee, I turned and snatched our backpack, then sprinted in the opposite direction. As Jay followed behind me, he wheezed, or maybe it was a sort of sob. A bug flew into my mouth. The swamp closed its thick, green curtain around us—a finale, no encore —and I ignored the shouts of the Zimzee, the booming discharge of the rifle, as noises from a restless but now irrelevant audience.

Chapter 18

Even when you think that you are probably going crazy, there are things to keep you busy. Once we were far away from the Zimzee, I started to count. The number of steps it took to reach the road: four hundred and two. The number before a car finally passed us: one thousand fifteen. The number of times I heard an unfamiliar bird cry, the number of littered Coke cans, the number of bug bites on my arms.

We must have looked terrible, even for Florida. No one stopped to give us a ride. Then again, it was me holding out my thumb, since Jay was too beat, and maybe that was the difference.

Neither of us were about to sleep out in the swamp again, so after dark, we found a neighborhood and snuck into some kids' treehouse, really just a platform of two-by-fours and a couple of beanbag chairs. I didn't say it to Jay, but I figured we were within screaming distance of a bunch of neighbors, if it came to another monster in the night.

"Dinner saved us," I said, the closest we'd come to broaching the incident. "I will never be afraid of an alligator again."

"Good old Dinner," Jay said from his beanbag chair. "I

miss hamburgers. We would eat hamburgers every Monday night."

My stomach jerked in its usual spasm of hunger. I wished that the sack of it would vanish so that I wouldn't have to think about its demands. If only my whole digestive system would disappear, then I wouldn't have to eat or slurp oily puddles of water or shit in the woods or use waxy leaves as toilet paper. "Do you think it's a Monday?"

Jay shrugged. "I miss jam. Jam on toast."

Stars winked from between the branches of the tree. They were like flakes of instant potatoes or granules of sugar; I could only think of food metaphors. "Remember that time we—the three of us—tried to make cupcakes for the class? It was my birthday."

"Yeah." Jay shifted and the wooden platform of the tree-house creaked. "But it wasn't your birthday. We were only going to tell the teacher that it was. And we were going to put weed in the cupcakes, get the whole class high. I wouldn't do a girl thing like *baking* unless there was weed."

I didn't remember any of that stuff; in my memory, the whole episode had been innocent. "No; you're wrong. We wanted to make vanilla with chocolate frosting. Where would we have gotten weed?"

"Toshi knew some guy, he said. But of course he didn't really, and he brought us oregano or some shit, and the cupcakes came out tasting awful."

I closed my eyes, trying hard to see things the way Jay had seen them. "I thought we were just bad at baking. That we messed up the recipe."

"That's okay, Bennet. You never had any idea what was really going on. Like you blind yourself on purpose."

"What are you talking about?" Jay was starting to piss me off. "I have a great memory. An elephant memory. For reals."

"Whatever you need to tell yourself."

We lay there in silence for a long time, and I thought that

Jay had probably fallen asleep and that maybe I should pinch him or whisper something nightmare-inducing into his ear for being such an off-target dick about my memory, but then he spoke.

"You think he'll tell the Eye Whites what we did?"

Of course he was talking about the Zimzee. That same anxiety I'd quelled earlier by counting everything started to swell in my throat. A low-grade panic had followed me ever since that last time in New Veronia, and the constant dread was wearing me down.

Night had buried the twilight; the only things I could see to count were the stars; after I'd done them, I started counting up things from my memory, like the houses on my street, the rotating meals served in the high school cafeteria, every single friend I'd ever had—that last number wasn't big —and then I subtracted Toshi. Tosh was gone.

"If he tells, that ruins all my plans," Jay said. "They'll think I'm sick. That something is wrong with me. But maybe they wouldn't believe him, or I could kill him."

I punched the beanbag chair I was sitting on, and I was surprised at how good it felt, so I punched the floor. The hard wood of the treehouse balked my fist. "Toshi is *gone*. You're so upset about what that Zimzee man did to us, and look at what we did to Tosh. Basically, we're no better than him." The reverberation of my punches shuddered through my body, and something about the frequency of the vibration uncoiled the cold, dark portion of my brain inside which I had stored the details of that night with Toshi. Once the memory was freed, I'd never be able to stuff it back.

"Don't you fucking compare me to that swamp monster," Jay said. "If you can't see the difference, you're crazier than I thought."

"Fuck you," I said, because he had to be feeling the same icy burn of shame and guilt that I did; I couldn't handle the burden of being alone in this.

Jay curled up into his beanbag chair and, after a while, his breathing steadied into sleep. I felt exhausted, too, but my mind raced; I couldn't relax. Something was bothering me, something about what we'd done to Toshi and what had happened afterward. I had this image of Tosh hanging from a rope like the one the Zimzee had tied around Dinner, hanging from a tree right over the spot our crew used to stand before school, but that couldn't be a real memory... or maybe I'd seen it on the news? My head throbbed.

The black backpack sat like a shadow at Jay's feet. Carefully, quietly, I eased it over to my side of the treehouse and dug through its contents to find the note that Toshi had left for Jay. It was zipped carefully inside an interior pouch meant to hold pens and pencils. I waited a long time for my eyes to adjust to the dark, and then I read.

Jay—

I had to do this, to kill myself, because I couldn't stand it anymore. The way Bennet and you embarassed me was the worst. I would never be able to live this down, so I have to end it. I can't live another day.

Toshi

With a growing apprehension, I read it again, and a third time, until something clicked. *Embarassed.* That was the problem: it should have had double R's. Toshi had been amazing at English; even under duress, he never would have misspelled this word. The handwriting looked pretty much like Toshi's, but maybe it had been copied from something else Toshi had written. If the note was a fake, then Jay must have lied to me, but I couldn't understand why. There was some huge flaw in the way I'd pieced everything together. All the things I thought I knew—about Toshi, about Jay, about my dad and mom, even about myself—kept shifting, when they should have stayed fixed in place, frozen in memory. I pressed against my forehead in a feeble attempt to fit me back together.

Holding the note, I straddled Jay in his beanbag chair so

that he couldn't escape. "What is this?" I said as he startled awake. "Toshi didn't write this note. Did you write it? Is he even dead?"

Jay's body trembled beneath me. "What are you talking about?" he said.

I punched him in the side of the head in the stagey way I'd learned in theater, not to hurt him, just to let him know I needed answers. "Tell me," I said.

It sounded like all the night animals and insects had fallen silent to give Jay's words more room. Someone was burning trash far off and the dirty smell tendriled faintly through the tree branches.

Jay closed his eyes, making his whole face a shadow. "I don't know what you're talking about."

I plugged him again, this time to make his ears ring.

Jay popped his jaw and then said, "I guess I wrote it."

Even through my fury, I marveled: Jay was a brilliant actor, to have made me believe that Toshi was dead; with his skills, I would have landed the lead in every school play. I wanted to shove the paper down his throat, but it was better to preserve his offense. "If Toshi is alive, why did we run away? What did we *do* all this for?"

"The stuff we did to him that night," Jay said, "he wanted it."

"No," I said, "what we did was evil. Just like that man we ended up with. Worse. Toshi was crying, he said no…"

Jay tried to sit up, but I kept him pinned.

"You don't get it," he said. "Toshi and me, we'd been doing that for months. Getting off that way. He *wanted* me to do it. It was weird: he liked it. But maybe that night was too much, because he got mad, and when I found him the next morning, he started threatening me, said he would tell the whole school…" Jay's hot breath repelled me.

"Toshi was going to tell everyone at school? You were… for *months*?"

"You don't understand... he was different... hairless... they are over there, where there are less women, and this is a thing, they do this to each other over there, so they've become more woman-like, and it was just something we did, kind of like I was fucking any other girl."

Small bursts of light popped in front of my eyes, and I couldn't tell if they were fireflies or my synapses firing. "And he was okay with it? When you did that?" I thought about Toshi sneaking into Stella's room; he'd stuck my cock in his mouth without any cajoling from me. Maybe what Jay had made me do to Toshi hadn't been completely evil.

"But that last morning, when I went back to my house, to get supplies before we went hitchhiking, he was waiting for me in my room. I don't know how he got in there. But he had proof, he had evidence about what him and me had been doing together, and he was going to tell. So that's why we had to go far away."

"That's why we ran away. Not because of the police or juvie or anything like that. Not because Toshi killed himself."

"Toshi was always the woman. I mean, that's the only way we did it. But even so, my dad would murder me. If Toshi told, my dad would hear about it, and I'd be dead for sure."

My emotions were tangible; they were choking me. "*You* made up his suicide," I said. "*You* wrote the note." Inside of me whirled fear and disbelief and anger and self-hatred and jealousy, too. I felt jealous that Jay and Toshi had carried on this secret relationship without me, that they had excluded me from the group. It was crazy to feel jealous about this, but I did, and I knew that I would have to punish Jay for it.

"It was him or me," Jay said. "My dad would've lynched me. This was the best thing I could think of." He sounded like he was practically begging me. Jay needed me, I saw now. This whole trip, he'd been getting weaker, and I'd been picking up his slack. "With Toshi gone like this," he said, "you and me could move on; I wanted to make it easier for you, this way it was easier to forget him. It was his fault we had to run off: first he asked for it, but then he snapped. I don't know why. It wasn't our fault."

After a while, my racing heart slowed; I made a decision: it was so much easier to agree with Jay on this rather than to accept that I was a monster.

We woke in the dark to a woman screaming up at us.

"What are you two tramps *doing* up there?" she said. "Beat it, before I call the sheriff."

We scrambled down from the tree and loped off, the woman's shouts following us all the way like ghostly pronouncements of my own discontent: *delinquents, foul-smelling, going to have to* burn *those bean bags*.

The town we'd stumbled into was a scattering of houses with a couple of stores, a diner, and a bail bond place. It was maybe an hour till sunrise, and everything was shut tight except the twenty-four hour bail bond store, where a jaundiced light glowed through the glass door. A phone booth stood on the corner, but when I shut myself inside, I found the cord that should have been attached to the phonebook cut and dangling. Rage bubbled up in me; Jay and I hadn't been given even a shred of luck. I kicked the glass door of the booth in frustration, but it only opened compliantly to usher me out.

Jay had been standing on the sidewalk watching me. "Got a quarter? I think you could use that to call the operator. She could look up your mom's number."

"No, Jay," I said, talking right up into his face, "I don't have a quarter, since all our money was *stolen*." I hooked my thumbs behind the straps of the backpack. It was mine now; Jay's lies had gotten us into this mess, had tricked me into running away, and so now everything would be on my terms. "Do *you* have a quarter? Jay? Do you?"

He shook his head no; his breath came shallow. He said, "Your eyes are all weird. What are you going to do?" He sounded scared.

Jay's fear coursed through me like a drug: it made me feel sort of invincible, the way I figured Jay usually felt. Maybe I had somehow stolen that power from him when we'd fucked, like all his greatness had been absorbed into me. "We aren't going to be able to get anywhere without money," I said. At this hour, the whole world was deserted; no one would see what I was about to do.

The plan must have started percolating in my head as soon as we'd walked down the dinky main drag of town, and now it began to solidify, to knit together out of the air, to fill me with self-importance, but the reality of the idea was somehow fake, too, like I was no longer the real me, but a me inside of a play, a *better* me, and the plot had already been written: now all I had to do was fulfill it. I kept one hand in my pocket, closed over the gun, as the other reached out to open the door of the bail bond store.

A man stood behind a counter in a white shirt and string tie. He was reading a book, but when we entered, he flipped it words-down to mark his place. On the cover, a couple of cowboys rode horses into a blood-red sunset.

"Howdy, boys," he said. "What can I do you for?"

"A Mexican," Jay said under his breath.

I pushed the hatred out through my pores, coating my whole body with a glimmering armor of loathing. Under this protection I could do what needed doing.

"Give us your money," I said. Beside me, Jay buzzed like a hundred thirty pounds of pure nervy energy; I willed him to look fierce. "Hand it over to this guy here"—I bent my head towards Jay—"and we'll get out of your hair. Or don't, and there'll be consequences."

The man's hands were palms-down on the counter. "Now boys," he said. "Your pops just get thrown in jail, maybe? You need to make bail for him?"

"Don't move those hands unless it's to get the money."

"Boys, now, listen: we don't keep the funds on the premises. I'm sorry to inform you. We just wire a promise on over to the courthouse."

"Give it over," I said. "I know you got money in here."

"I'm telling you," the man said. "You should have thought this through."

"I have a gun!" I said. "I have a fucking gun!" The rage I'd felt earlier in the phone booth surged up again, swelling every one of my veins. It roiled beneath my skin. "Now," I said, and, "goddamnit," and "if you don't, I will…"

The man's lips rose into sort of a goofy smile. "It's the truth."

I brought the gun up above the level of the counter, and the man's features slackened. He reached for me, but before he could get to me, I pulled the trigger. The release felt so good that I pulled it again.

As blood webbed out across his white shirt, his eyes rolled downwards to take in the wound, or maybe to look for his western, to see if he could just go back to reading like we'd never come into his shop, and before he buckled, before he fell, I pressed the gun into Jay's hand. "You shoot him, too," I said. "This isn't only my fault."

Jay shook his head.

"Goddammit you do it *now!*"

He shivered and leaned over the counter—the man had dropped into an awkward pile on the floor—to put a bullet straight through the body's throat. I snatched the gun back.

"Where's the money in this fucking place," I said as I searched behind the counter. Pieces of paper spilled from a drawer; paperbacks were stuck everywhere. But there was no money. I kicked the water cooler and threw a calculator against the wall; there wasn't even a cash register. As I stepped over the body, I thought about snatching its bolo tie or wallet, but everything was covered in blood. The sewer smell churned my stomach. "Let's go," I said, and then Jay and I swung through into the too-early air, pumping ourselves up and out and into the next life, the one where we did better, where everything came easy and we were happy.

Chapter 19

"I don't want to go so far back," Jay told me.

We were in the swamp, hiding out. "I heard sirens," I said. "If I can still hear them, they can still find us."

Jay feared whatever might be secreted in the swamp, but we were the ones using it for cover, now; it was the only place where we'd be safe. "We've become real outlaws," I said. "Not like before, with Toshi. This time, we really did something."

Jay was scared to follow me, but he was afraid to be on his own even more, and so he trailed me like a dog.

"People live in here," I said. "They do it, so we can do it too. At least for a while. They'll be looking for us at my mom's, I think. Maybe even have road blocks. We'll have to wait a while before we go to her. But the swamp—the swamp is for people like us."

"Could be no one saw us go into that place," Jay said.

"We're suspect." Jay seemed to be getting stupider and stupider with age. "You're the one who said that being on the move keeps you from getting caught."

When the day started to fade towards dusk, we found a good sleeping tree, this thing that had a huge trunk made up of a hundred smaller trunks. We crawled up there and rested among the branches. "Figure out some plants for us to eat," I said. Earlier, we'd swallowed some raw eggs that we'd found in a nest, but we needed more in order to keep going.

"You want to sleep in a tree again?"

"This time," I said, "I won't leave the gun behind like an idiot. Hurry up; I'm hungry."

"I don't know any of the plants around here," Jay said. "Maybe I could hunt us some food." He stared at the gun in my lap.

"No way." I wasn't so naïve as to hand him the gun at this point, when he was starting to realize that our roles were changing; I wrapped both hands around it, ready to fight him if he tried to take it. But I shouldn't have worried: of course he did what I wanted; he couldn't turn against me. I was the new Jay, now. I was in charge.

When the dark came, I couldn't get to sleep because of an empty gnawing deep inside my middle. The ground rustled, and not too far off, something splashed in shallow water. The dark was never quite full, as if half the swampy things phosphoresced.

But Jay could sleep anywhere. After he'd been snoring for a while, I brought out Stella's panties and fitted them to my hand; I rubbed the slippery material across my face to feel something nice for a change. "Are you okay?" I asked, and the puppet said she was. She told me that she was proud I was taking over, because Jay had never been the leader, not the real leader, of our group. I breathed her in; her sweet smell grew fainter every day. "There's something in you, Bennet," Stella told me, "that's better than him. Remember what he did to you?"

"No," I said, "no."

"When you were kids? Nine years old?"

"No."

"Well, I do," the Stella puppet said. "You're ready to remember, now. Jay isn't all that powerful, not anymore."

Overhead, a cloud broke into jagged pieces around the sliver of moon. I couldn't stop this moment.

"He locked you into the closet," Stella said, "in our parents' room."

"I never went in there before recently. Before the day that I got you."

"And he told you that if you gave yourself away, our father would slice off your toes, one by one, and feed them to you."

"I don't remember this at all." Their bedroom, the rumpled and stained sheets, the weapons mounted on the walls, flashed through my mind. "It must not have happened."

"And so you sat in that closet for three hours, and in the last hour, you listened to them having sex, only you thought that maybe he was trying to rip off all her hair, and so you looked out where the closet door didn't quite meet the jamb."

A bit drilled into my head, plunging deep inside after the first half-inch of resistant skull. In the cave it made, a memory expanded. "I was terrified," I said, my head throbbing. Sex had looked like murder, like the intestines were spilling out of the woman's back end, and her cries had made my tonsils ache. The smell in that close space was not unlike the smell of the purple satin.

"You were terrified. You pissed yourself."

"Only because I had to stay in the closet. I couldn't get to a bathroom."

"No. That's why they called you Soppy."

"Is it?"

"Because Jay told the whole school."

I pressed the purple fabric to my eyes.

"That's how it has always been with Jay," was the last thing Stella ever said to me.

———

In the early morning, I sensed that they were closing in. I thought I heard the thud of booted feet and saw a glow from their flashlights.

"Jay," I said, "Jay, come on." I shook him awake and we moved off in the direction I thought best. Jay said he could feel his muscles getting thinner, and I told him to nut up.

We came upon an old shed, nothing else around. Its tin siding had rusted through in places. The shelter was a sign to me that I could handle our lives from now on: I had found the shed that would protect us.

Inside, it smelled like canned tuna about to turn. A small animal skeleton lay in one corner, but you couldn't see it after the door was shut.

"Bennet," Jay said.

"Whisper."

"What are we going to eat in here? There's nothing."

"It's only for a little while. I know exactly what we need to do."

"Okay—what?"

"Tell me something." I sat down and dug my fingers into the shed's dirt floor. The press of the ground beneath my nails felt good, like wiggling a loose tooth: that piece of you about to pop. "Was it you who told everyone at school to call me Soppy?"

Jay huffed air through his mouth, and then he spoke cautiously, as if he were answering a teacher. "You know that I did. You were right there. Everyone thought it was funny. I mean, don't you remember?"

And the problem was that I did remember, now. That memory had unwound itself into a cold ribbon in my brain;

it floated around the new space inside my skull, bumping up against the memory of Toshi that final night in New Veronia and of the bolo tie man's body unfurling from its life.

"Is that why you think I'm not good enough for your stupid family?" I said. "Why you wanted to keep me and Stella apart? Well, what do you think about me now?"

Jay said, "That was forever ago. It was nothing. Are you mad at me or something?"

"Mad?" I said. "Why would I be mad? I just fucking hate you." I waited a beat, imagining Jay's taut face in the darkness of the shed. "Just joshing." The fear and anger and frustration had built up inside me like gunpowder, and I was itching to go off, itching again for that quick click of the trigger to release me: Jay would give me that, I knew. It was only a matter of time.

"Joshing?" he said. "Ha."

———

We slept in the shed at opposite ends of the floor—I made Jay take the half with the tiny skeleton—and I dreamed that I had to lift my hands, I had to hold up my hands because someone was changing me into a clean shirt. It felt cool against my irritated skin. Then I returned to wakefulness and realized that a huge voice, magnified by a megaphone, was telling us to come out with our hands up.

I had been waiting for this moment; it was like I'd created it with my waiting. My whole body pounded in excitement: they would never capture me. I crawled over to Jay and put my hand around the back of his neck.

"I have a hostage in here!" I yelled. "Don't you come one step closer, or he's dead!"

Jay's neck tensed. "What are you doing?" he said. "Is this part of the plan?"

"You're my sacrifice," I told him. "You're the reason

everything went wrong for me in Delaware from the very start. I would have been fine, if not for you. I would have been happy. I would never have been Soppy, never done all the stupid stuff that I did with you."

"What are you talking about, Bennet?" he said. "We're best friends."

"Surrender," a voice said. "Surrender now."

"It's your fault we're out here," I said. "You forced me to run away with you because you were scared, because you were a faggot with Toshi and you were scared of your father and you couldn't face yourself."

Jay recoiled as if I'd hit him. "I'm not," he said. "Come on. We're best friends."

"No, we're not." I punched open the shed's door with my foot and prodded Jay out first; I pressed the gun between two knobs of his spine. Something ripe and gaseous gurgled from him.

"I wasn't kidding!" I said to the blinding sun. When the dazzle faded from my eyes, I saw about five uniformed figures peering out at us from behind trees.

I aimed the gun and shot Jay in the thigh.

As I ran, Jay's agonized screams echoed. He would distract them; he would let me get away. The one or two officers who had set off after me were too fat, they were falling behind, and so they pulled out their weapons to try and stop me, but I couldn't be stopped, the bullets they discharged skittered feebly through the air, they were far behind, yards and yards behind me, and as I hurtled over a decaying trunk, I smelled freedom on the other side.

But I landed face-first into the loam: my toe had caught on a root.

Chapter 20

When they delivered me to jail, my fingerprints matched up to the ones taken after we'd been booked into the Dover station for piss-bombing the jocks' party, so they knew my name, where I was from, everything. The gun had my fingerprints and Jay's, and they could match the bullets right to us. No one ever mentioned that first burglary at the Mobil station, though, or the episode with Toshi that spurred us to skip town in the first place.

They wouldn't tell me where they'd locked up Jay, I guess so we wouldn't collude on our eventual trial, or possibly so I couldn't finish the job I'd started by shooting him in the leg. He might've been chumming it up with the Eye Whites, or just as likely he was alone and frightened and always watching his back. In jail, most of the guys did gravitate towards people with the same color skin as them, so maybe this made Jay feel at home; maybe jail was as close as he'd ever get to that world he'd wanted.

The endless summer of Florida, which I glimpsed sometimes through the chain link, was a cruel stagnation that reminded me of our months building New Veronia, before everything got so screwed up, before I was granted my wish to never see Jay again. When I could, I avoided reminders, like the woodworking shop onsite; I couldn't bring myself to enter it because I knew that even the purr of a saw against wood, a feeling I had once enjoyed, would mean nothing but New Veronia to me now.

I thought about writing Toshi to check in, to prove to myself that he was truly still alive, but he'd become a distant memory, as was the kid I'd been when we were friends. It didn't really matter to me anymore if he was dead or not, since that part of my life had been packed away and shipped off to a place I'd never get to visit.

The facility contacted my mother about my predicament, and after I added her to my list of visitors, she arrived on a bright afternoon in winter. Her hair was dyed in an obvious sort of way, with evenly spaced strips of blond in among the brown, and her face was a long oval when I'd remembered it as a heart.

"Mom," I said as she sat across from me at the folding table. Signs everywhere said No Touching, and there was a picture, too, for the illiterates.

"I am so disappointed in you," was the first thing she said to me in thirteen years.

"I was coming to find you," I said.

"I would have turned you over to the police straight-away." Her eyelashes were pale and stubby; I wondered if she'd cried off her mascara on the trip here.

"But before all this, you wanted me to come live with you in Florida, right? So that we could spend some time together?"

"None of this is my fault. I've been praying for you, but of course that fails if you're fated to wickedness in the first place."

She wore a ring on her third finger. Probably she'd replaced my dad and me as soon as she'd had the chance.

"What's your favorite food?" I asked.

Silent, she stared at the visitors beside us, a woman jiggling a fat-headed infant.

"Do you remember that time when I was a baby"—I covertly poked her hand so that she would look at me—"and you were changing my diaper, and I peed on you?"

"No."

"You were wearing the same necklace." It hung over the collar of her shirt. "A gold cross."

"Devin bought me this necklace for our fifth anniversary. I didn't have it back then."

The fat-headed baby started to hiccup.

I asked, "Did you leave us because Dad is a drunk?"

She didn't move; she didn't blink. She said, "You're like the more extreme version of him. I feel that you're trying to convince me of something, but I don't know what it is."

"I haven't heard from him," I said, "Dad."

The baby opened its gummy mouth to chew on its own fingers.

She said, "He thought that if you two were apart for a little while, then maybe you'd both get back to yourselves. It had gone too far, though; I wouldn't have been able to make any difference."

. . .

My stomach groaned from the recent assault of a mess hall lunch. "He asked you to take me? You didn't think up the idea yourself?"

"These things are complicated."

"Why did you come to see me?" I asked.

She made a soft noise like a bird dying. "I needed to remind myself that I don't know you."

The windows in the visiting room were much larger than the one in my cell. A patch of sun on the floor had almost reached my foot.

"None of this came from me," she said. "I would never be able to produce a... a killer."

"Alleged."

Finally, she looked into my face. "I'm not coming back here."

"I know." It wasn't a huge loss. The visit was like finding a toy you'd misplaced years before, a toy you had missed like crazy when it had first disappeared, but that you had outgrown in the interim.

She stood to leave. "Don't contact me. Never again."

"I know."

Since her, no one has visited me.

Boredom is like a mirror that refuses to reflect anything back: you look into it and look into it, expecting, but you only see an unbroken emptiness that should be filled with life. That's how boredom and loneliness are similar: I used to think that loneliness was just emptiness, but now I know that loneliness is an absence where you feel sure something should be. Boredom and loneliness, they're both mirrors that refuse to reflect, no matter what you put in front of them.

⸻

It's incredible how long they can hold you in jail before you're even brought to trial. I think I've been here twenty-two months, maybe. My public defender waived time in order, he said, to give us a while longer to get my defense together, but he's got dawdling down to an art form, if he's working on my case at all. Truthfully, it doesn't matter much to me, because the prison they'll send me to will be worse: higher security, crappier meals, more desperate people. I guess there's still a chance I could be freed, but not much of one. I've come around to the idea that an excellent memory might be more of a detriment in the real world, and so I keep telling them that it wasn't me, that I would never kill a man, that I would be able to remember if I had, but they don't seem to doubt my guilt. Plus, they stuck me with attempted murder for the bullet I put in Jay, a crime that had too many pig witnesses to even think about denying.

After a while in here, when my mind started to feel like my jail cell—empty, cold, echoing—I asked if they would bring me some Shakespeare. The CO came back and handed me a bible, saying that was the closest they had. It felt like some kind of unfunny joke, reminding me about my mother and her Catholicism and maybe if I hadn't turned away from that church, or if my mother hadn't turned away from me, I wouldn't be here. But maybe not; you never know. Then I began to flip through the pages. Several different types of handwriting had left messages in the margins: *2 benzos/2 oxies 17B, Clay Johnston sux dick, 10 cartons bounty on Raneek Lowes head.* That gave me the idea, I guess: all those tissue-thin pages, the big margins, the nothing else to do. It all started with New Veronia, I know that much. It was Jay's idea.

In the summer of New Veronia, I still had total belief in my own memory, but now that I've written pretty much to the end of it, my perfect recall has been unveiled as faulty. I tried to put everything down true to how I felt at the time, in the moment, because memory shouldn't be tainted by what happened after, but I'm starting to think that I've been pushing for an impossible purity. Sometimes I look back at the margins and feel like it happened differently, or I wonder if Jay would tell it the same way, or a particular biblical word, *rapturous, omnipotent, betrothed*, not really my word, makes it into my retelling. I even copped an illustration of tigers from Matthew 23:12, comparing it to Jay only after the fact. And if there are different versions, different ways of getting the story across, then which one is true? Alone in my bunk, when I hear Toshi squealing, when I see the string tie cinched too tight around the man's throat, are those exact imprints from reality, or have they been altered by my guilt?

I'm worried what will happen to me, to my brain, now that this writing and doodling will no longer occupy it, now that the story is all down in pen and it's likely that nothing much will change for me ever again. The years of my future stretch stagnant and unending, so I carry this book around wherever it's allowed, which has had unexpected consequences: the other inmates call me Bible Boy, and I think that's what keeps them from messing with me too much— lots of the guys in here believe in a vengeful God. It's a neat trick, really, to have tucked my story, this reminder of my other life, into a book that everyone pretends to respect. If this had been Shakespeare, poor doomed Hamlet and King Lear and all the rest would be in tatters across the yard by now, and I'd sport perpetual black eyes for being a theater nerd. But instead I'm left in peace to scan the margins of my bible, and the words I've written there remind me that I had a different life, once, that a different life is possible. Being locked up, you can forget that too easily. So I stare at my handwriting getting smaller and more cramped near the back of the book, as I come closer to running out of room, and I try to accept that this will be my whole existence.

Jail is dehumanizing, of course it is, but the way they really get you is by keeping everything unchanged. Meal times, recreation times, announcements, hygiene. Can you be a real person if you never get to decide when to shower, or are you more like a character in a play who is obligated to shower in line thirteen of scene two, night after night, forever?

The thing that really bothers me is, if life in lockup is always the same, and lockup will be my life forever, then I'll never get to remember anything new, not ever again. The day I'm living will be the same as all the days before it, so instead of memories, they're just routines. But to never make another memory can be a comfort, too: the only way I'm able to fall asleep at night is to chant to myself, over and over, that this right here is my forever.

One of the saddest sights in my narrow world is the breakfast tray arriving through a slot in the metal door at exactly five minutes after six. Nine minutes later, when I'm brushing my teeth, I always do it hard enough to make my gums bleed, to prove to myself that blood is still leaking through my veins, because I feel emptied out, like nothing is inside of me and nothing good will come out of me ever again. But I guess it doesn't need to, seeing as my future is a huge pile of zilch.

The bars of my cell do this funny thing when you pace past them: they move together and apart, together and apart, and sometimes this gives me the idea that they can meld and melt, that they aren't as solid as everyone wants to think. But that's just looking: in my hands, they feel hard and cold as bone.

Acknowledgments

Thank you to my first and best reader, Will Cordeiro, and to Tiki "Dog" Coco for the lap warming. Also, thanks to Lawrence Lenhart for the idea and to Gavin Buckley and Jamison Crabtree for their manly insights.

Many thanks to my inspirational mentors at Cornell: Stephanie Vaughn, J. Robert Lennon, and Ernesto Quiñonez. Plus my MFA cohort, especially Laurel Lathrop, Tacey Atsitty, Benjamin Garcia, and Elizabeth Rogers.

And, of course, much gratitude to my eclectic Tucson workshop: Cybele Knowles and Ted McLoof. From my time at the University of Arizona, thank you to Donald Dunbar, Jason Brown, Manuel Muñoz, Matthew Rotando, and Elizabeth Evans. The University of Arizona Poetry Center will always be my favorite place to read—thank you to its dedicated staff and volunteers, and to Gail Browne for being the best boss.

I am indebted to Christian Soto, Andie Frances, Meredith Heller, Michelle Coe, Lara Bennett, and Christie Melnick for their support. Thank you to the Bushes and Cordeiros for acquainting me with Delaware. I am also grateful to the Averbachs and Les and Elana Hunter for a beautiful and inspirational summer space in which to write. Founding Coes, thank you for always keeping books in the house.

A huge thanks to Christoph Paul and Leza Cantoral for their editorial prowess and for wanting to publish this book in the first place, and to Matthew Revert for the excellent cover design.

About the Author

M. S. Coe has stories published in *Antioch Review*, *The Cantab-rigian*, *Electric Literature*, *Cosmonauts Avenue*, *jmww*, and else-where. Coe has completed writing residencies at Petrified Forest National Park, Herbert Hoover National Historic Site, and the Ora Lerman Trust's Soaring Gardens Artist Retreat. Coe, who is based in Flagstaff, Arizona, earned an MFA from Cornell University and acts as the co-editor of Eggtooth Editions.

Also by CLASH Books

TRAGEDY QUEENS: STORIES INSPIRED BY LANA DEL REY & SYLVIA PLATH

Edited by Leza Cantoral

GIRL LIKE A BOMB

Autumn Christian

CENOTE CITY

Monique Quintana

99 POEMS TO CURE WHATEVER'S WRONG WITH YOU OR CREATE THE PROBLEMS YOU NEED

Sam Pink

THIS BOOK IS BROUGHT TO YOU BY MY STUDENT LOANS

Megan J. Kaleita

HEXIS

Charlene Elsby

I'M FROM NOWHERE

Lindsay Lerman

NIGHTMARES IN ECSTASY

Brendan Vidito

PAPI DOESN'T LOVE ME NO MORE

Anna Suarez

ARSENAL/SIN DOCUMENTOS

Francesco Levato

FOGHORN LEGHORN

Big Bruiser Dope Boy

TRY NOT TO THINK BAD THOUGHTS

Art by Matthew Revert

SEQUELLAND

Jay Slayton-Joslin

JAH HILLS

Unathi Slasha

GIMME THE LOOT: STORIES INSPIRED BY NOTORIOUS B.I.G

Edited by Gabino Iglesias

THE HAUNTING OF THE PARANORMAL ROMANCE AWARDS

Christoph Paul & Mandy De Sandra

DARK MOONS RISING IN A STARLESS NIGHT

Mame Bougouma Diene

TRASH PANDA

Leza Cantoral

WE PUT THE LIT IN LITERARY

CLASHBOOKS.COM

FOLLOW

TWITTER

IG

FB

@clashbooks

EMAIL

clashmediabooks@gmail.com

Printed in the USA
CPSIA information can be obtained
at www.ICGtesting.com
JSHW022323140824
68134JS00019B/1269